THE SECRET'S OUT

CAROLINE SPRINGS CHARTER

LILA ROSE

Neringa Neringiukas
Thank you for your constant support.

PREQUEL

NANCY

*N*ancy Alexander placed her phone on the table. She looked down, but wasn't really focused on it. No, her mind was running over things from the phone call she just had.

Her youngest daughter, Josie, hadn't been home that Christmas holiday. In fact, she hadn't returned home in a long time and Nancy was worried. For the tenth time that day, she called her daughter's mobile demanding answers. Only it wasn't her daughter who supplied them.

Josie's housemate, where she lived in a small apartment close to her school, had answered.

"Mrs Alexander?" she whispered into the phone. Nancy should have realised then that something was wrong, but she didn't.

"Simone, honey, how many times do I have to tell you to call me Nancy? Now, can you tell me where my daughter is? I'm getting sick of this run around. She's either too busy to talk or on her way out somewhere. But I'm worried about my girl, Simone."

"You should be," Simone uttered and Nancy started to panic.

Nancy sat straight in her chair. "Tell me, Simone."

"It's not really my place."

"No, Simone, you tell me now so I can help."

"She won't want her mum here. That'll make things worse."

"Simone, tell me!"

"Josie's in the bathroom, but I can hear her crying. She cries a lot, Nancy, and I think it has to do with some guys who are hassling her. She's so quiet and timid. The stupid-heads find it fun to cause her problems."

"Is that all?" Nancy snapped in a hard tone.

"I-I think so? Please, please don't come here. I swear it'll make things worse."

"Oh, I won't come, darling. I'll be sending someone else."

"Who?"

"Doesn't matter. Just know help will be arriving soon, and watch over my girl 'til then."

"I will, Mrs–I mean, Nancy."

"Thank you, Simone, for telling me."

"I hate seeing Josie upset."

"I do also. I'm going to let you go now. I need to make a phone call."

Simone hung up the phone and not long after, Nancy stared at the phone on the table thinking. She picked it back up again and put it to her ear.

"Hello, my wonderful son-in-law."

"Nancy," was all Talon said.

"Josie is having trouble as school. Some guys are... annoying her, Talon." Usually, Nancy would taunt him to get a rise, but she wasn't in the mood, and she knew her son-in-law could tell by her tone.

"Fuck," Talon growled low. "I'll handle it."

"Good," Nancy said and hung up.

CHAPTER ONE

JOSIE

*L*ife on my own wasn't what I thought it would be. Two years of living away from home was getting to me. Two years of independence, two years of finding myself was... hard. Harder than I pictured. Sure, I found myself... in a way. Sure, I had independence. I had a job, had a great friend, and a roof over my head. Still, all I wanted was to be home. Be with the family who had opened their arms wide for me. They had adopted me, regardless of how troubled I was. I missed my sister, Zara, my brother, Matthew, but especially my mum and dad. I even missed my brothers-in-law, the goofy one, Julian, and the sometimes scary one, Talon. Most of all, I missed my nieces and nephews. Their light had helped me through many dark times. They were young and didn't know the real world could be scary. It was their excitement over little things that I appreciated and missed.

Which was why I had stayed away from home so many times over the past two years, because if I went there, I knew I'd want to stay and never leave again. I'd want to be back in *their* world, their open arms and the protection they provided me each and every day. I'd want to be surrounded in it all once more and forever. Never leaving again.

However, I had to stay strong.

I wanted to prove to them, and especially myself, I was able to live in the real world. No matter how scared I was each day, or how my brain screamed at me to stop the ridiculousness and get home. And no matter how much I hated living through the taunting and teasing each day for the past year, my decision was resolute.

Since *they* found out I was petrified of most men, of human contact, it had all changed.

The first time it happened they enjoyed the reaction they got from me. They thrived on the fact that it unnerved me.

Since then, it happened all the time, just so they could see me cower and cringe.

I was lucky to have found Simone, the sweet girl with shoulder-length black hair and dark blue eyes. It was as though fortune had rained down on me when it was Simone who answered the same ad I had two years earlier. It was an ad in the local paper I'd found before I moved to Melbourne, for two house guests to look after a fully furnished home while the owner travelled for business. When the owner was home, we rarely saw him. He tended to stay in the master bedroom. He was quiet and kept to himself, like me.

The idea of living my life as the local cat lady or hermit had been promising, for the first few months after I had moved in, which was possibly why Simone took it upon herself to get me out and about. She was determined for me to start living my life the way an eighteen-year-old should after flying the nest.

She showed me there was hope, kindness and love in the world outside of my family.

Simone was a great friend, the best anyone could have, trusting, loyal and bubbly. She took me under her wing and showed me how to get drunk, do shots, and dance until my legs wanted to fall from my body, just so they could rest. Dancing was fun.

At least I had that first year respite at uni before my new hell started. Even then, I kept to my shy self, still forming the knowledge of how people went about their day, how they communicated in the different way I was with my family. If it weren't for Simone, I would have been on my own, and surviving would have been the wrong term.

Everything had been okay... until Cameron Peterson took an interest in me.

At first, I thought he was different.

I thought he was nice.

I'd been wrong on so many levels.

To start off, he *had* been nice, sweet even. He saw that I was shy, so he approached me slowly and with caution. He said kind things to me and didn't invade my comfort zone.

But things must have been moving too slow for him, because after one weekend, a weekend where we saw each other out at a club, he changed.

He thought he owned me.

He thought I wanted him.

He had been wrong and he didn't like it.

The night we were out, he was drunk, and he was a mean drunk. I knew that because once he spotted me on the dance floor, he stalked over to me with a feral glint in his eyes, or so Simone explained afterwards when she watched his approach. His hands went straight to my waist. I flinched and tried to move away, but his grip tightened. My breath caught in my throat. For a moment, all but a second, I was scared it was David. The man who took so many things from me, most of all, my innocence. Even though I knew the sudden thought was ridiculous as he was dead, I couldn't stop the fear seeping into my body. I stiffened as Cameron rubbed his arousal into my backside. Simone, sensing my fear, like she did every time, came forward and pushed Cameron back. I hadn't told Simone of my past; however, she only had to watch me, like any other, to see that I was new to physical contact from people I didn't know. She always did her best to steer people away from me, no matter the situation and slowly, she was teaching me not all contact was bad. Not when it came from people I knew and trusted, so when she hugged me, I only flinched a little when it would startle me. I turned to see Cameron sneer at Simone, until he noticed I was watching and changed his expression to a lusty, drunken smile.

"Hey, baby," he said.

I cringed. "I-I'm not your baby, Cameron."

"Sure you are." He reached for me again. I backed up a step, my hands out in front of me. "Don't be like that." He chuckled.

In a loud enough voice so he could hear me over the pumping music, I said, "I'd prefer it if you didn't touch me, please."

He rolled his eyes. "Don't be stupid, Jo-Jo, you know you want me. I see the way you look at me." Lightning fast, he reached out and snagged my wrist, dragging me forward so our chests collided.

"Don't. Please, don't, you're drunk. I'll talk to you tomorrow," I pleaded and tried to pry myself away. Simone stepped up next to us trying to get Cameron off me, but he wouldn't have it. They started yelling at each other.

Tears formed, and just as quickly, they rolled down my cheeks, leaving a wet trail behind. There was no way to stop the whirlwind of emotions wreaking havoc inside my body. Spotting my tears, Cameron wiped them away. Ignoring Simone, he leaned toward me to get my attention. "You want me, Jo-Jo, like all the girls do. No one says no to me." Then he slammed his lips down on mine. I struggled and fought against him, but nothing worked, so when he shoved his tongue inside my mouth, I bit him.

Pushed away by strong hands, I stumbled into Simone. She wrapped her arms around my waist to steady me. "You stupid jerk," Simone screamed. People started taking notice. I was surprised they hadn't beforehand, though most were drunk and in their own little worlds. Some looked too scared to say or do anything. I couldn't blame them. I would have been the same.

"You stupid bitch," he snarled at me. He wiped his mouth and studied me. Whatever he saw had him smirking. "You really hate it, don't you? Touching, attention. Here I thought you were just shy, now I know you have mental problems." He chuckled. "Makes it more fun for me." He winked, turned, and walked away.

From that night on, he became my personal nightmare. I was terrified by his obsession with me.

He'd show up wherever I was. His eyes travelled along with every step I took. His smirk turned sexual and his words sinister. He wanted me, but he couldn't have me, and he didn't like that at all. So much so, if he couldn't make it to me during the day, he'd have his friends do his job for him and they'd follow me. I could hear their fake whispered conversations of how strange I was. They'd call me names like tease, slut and ugly.

All I wanted was to be left alone.

However, they wouldn't. They were puppets following their master's lead.

Once, six months ago, I even tried to go on a date with a shy guy like me. I could tell he was nervous. He didn't even make a move to hold my hand, which I liked. It went well, until Cameron showed up at the café. He slid into the booth opposite me, next to my date, and told him that I was a cock tease, that I had problems, and was mentally unstable. He warned my date that if he continued to date me, I would turn into a stalker, like I had with him. Apparently, Cameron was just following the 'bro code'. All men had to stick together and warn each other of the freaks, like me.

Of course, because my date was worried it was true and the fact that he didn't want Cameron's attention, he fled the café and I never saw him again.

After that, Cameron went from standing back and teasing, to touching. Any chance he got, he would rub up against me, run his hand down my back. Pretend to lean in to kiss me or tap me on the shoulder and yell, "Boo." Again, if he couldn't be around to do it, he'd have his friends fill in for him.

Every day I was a nervous wreck.

I'd become a jittery fool, one who was even more timid and withdrawn than I'd been after Zara and Talon saved me from David.

I was losing hope in society once more. I knew Simone saw it. I knew she was worried about me, but there was nothing I could do. I couldn't go to the police. I didn't want the attention, and I knew Cameron would make my life worse than it already was.

My grades declined, and once more my social skills took a hit. I was like a zombie walking around campus, with my head low, my books to my chest and a hunched posture, all while I waited for hell to begin for the day.

Even my boss, a fifty-year-old woman named Marybeth noticed the change in me. I'd lost count of how many times she had asked me if I was okay. All I could do was nod. Thankfully, due to my 'shyness', she had taken me off floor duty, from serving customers. Instead, I was out back helping with the preparation of the food and washing the dishes. I loved her for it. She knew I struggled being around strangers. At first, she'd encouraged me to try floor duty and for a while there, I loved it because I didn't have to touch anyone, and I only had to speak a few words... until everything went pear-shaped because of Cameron.

Misery was my name and I didn't know how to change it.

I wanted to reach out to my parents, my sister or brother even, but I didn't. Why? Because I felt I needed to deal with it on my own. It was my choice to move away. It was my choice to attend university, to be independent. If I ran home, if I rang them crying about how terrible it all was, I would be a failure. I couldn't become *that* person. I needed to show, not only myself, but my family, that I had grown. Their protection and their love had contributed to my freedom and independence. I was no longer that little girl who was carried from a nightmare. At least, I didn't feel I was. No matter what I was enduring every day and no matter how much it hurt, strength grew inside of me.

Still, I missed my family with every fibre of my being, missed their warmth and protection.

Because of that, everything hurt.

Simone tried her best to make me happy, get me to laugh, and for her, I did as best as I could.

I knew that when I smiled or laughed at her jokes, it didn't show in my eyes. There was no fooling her either; she would see through my façade every time, causing her to sigh in defeat. But she never gave up. The next day, she would make another attempt. I loved her for trying so much.

I stopped doing anything other than classes or work. As soon as class or my shift finished, I would race home. I was lucky I didn't live far from both places.

Cameron showed up many times at home. If Simone was home, she'd send him away. If she wasn't, I'd sit on the floor in the corner of the living room to listen and wait until he eventually left. I'd never caved and opened the door to him. If I did, the outcome wouldn't be pretty. His foul language and anger was enough to convince me he was a threat. It was that anger that would be taken out on me physically, destroying what little hope I had of ever finding normalcy.

About two months earlier his nightly visits finally stopped. One night when he came by, Parker, the owner, was home. He must have had a very bad business trip because when Cameron banged on the door, Parker swung my bedroom door open. The force from it hit my wall, causing me to squeal and jump. Parker stood in the doorway scowling. He then demanded to know if the loser at the door was annoying me. All I could do was nod. I was too terrified to do anything else. Once I answered, Parker then barked out, "Never be scared of me." I gave another nod and then he added, "I'll deal with it." He closed my door with a bang and stomped off toward the front door.

I wished I had the courage to have seen what occurred at the front door, all I heard was yelling, mainly from Parker. After a few noises, which sounded like punches, things fell silent and Parker was at my door again opening it. "He won't come here again. If he troubles you at other places, you need to find someone to deal with it." With that, he closed my door, gently that time, and went back to his room, leaving me with yet more questions regarding my housemate. All I knew was that he looked to be around twenty-four, and he travelled a lot; though I wasn't sure he liked what he did.

If it wasn't for the day he handled Cameron, I would have kept on thinking he was a nerdy bookworm with how he stayed locked in his room reading with his sexy glasses on his nose. I had seen he was a fan of reading when one day I'd been walking past his room, his door suddenly opened and he stepped out. I looked over his shoulder quickly to see his walls were lined with bookcases and *many* books sat upon them. However, the way he handled my trouble at the front door had me second guessing myself. Parker had been true to his word though. Cameron never darkened our doorstep again. Though, it hadn't changed the attention I still got at uni. If anything, whatever Parker did caused Cameron's stare to turn deadly.

After that incident, Parker stayed around for two more days before he left again. We said nothing to each other about what had happened. Even when he returned two weeks later to stay another three nights, zilch was shared between us. Since then, he hadn't been back. I couldn't help but pray he was okay.

Simone, knowing something had changed, asked me why Cameron wasn't coming to the house any longer. I told her about Parker. Her eyes glazed over and she got a small, satisfied smile on her face. "Now we just need to find someone to do whatever he did in public when dickface is screwing with you," she'd said.

Standing in the bathroom, I shook all thoughts from my mind, my eyes were still red from crying in the shower. I waited in the bathroom trying to hide it from Simone. I took a deep breath and swiped at the fogged-up mirror to stare at my reflection.

I'd lost weight, enough for me to know that I was under-weight. My cheek bones jutted out and my once shiny styled hair looked lifeless, so did the bags under my eyes. I lifted my red waves and let them fall back into the wet mess it was. Simone had surprised me on my twentieth birthday, just four months earlier, with a beauty day.

I'd been reluctant to go due to my phobias. Still, because Simone was such a great supportive friend, I sucked it up for the day and went out with her to get my nails painted black and my long, very curly, red hair was styled into a modern wave. Something I absolutely loved. It was too bad it looked lifeless once again, even when dried. What didn't help was my lack of care.

My mum had been ecstatic when I sent her a picture of my hair. She'd gushed over it and told me how beautiful I was.

God, I missed her.

People were right. Home was where the heart is, because mine had never left Ballarat. My heart stayed with my family, only making an appearance sometimes when

Simone brought it out in me. Any other day I was lifeless, a shell.

Maybe I was being overly dramatic, maybe I could go home and not think I was a failure.

Honestly, I didn't know what to do.

I didn't know because I stopped thinking a while ago.

I stopped feeling.

All that mattered were the grades I needed.

At least there was still that tiny spark inside of me that wanted the future career I longed for so long ago.

Currently, that was the only thing that kept me here, that kept me from running back to my family.

I often wondered if I had someone to care for me back then, maybe I would have noticed David's attention was more than fatherly. Perhaps I would have seen that he was nothing more than a dirty old man lusting for a minor. If someone had been there for me, I wouldn't have been beaten, broken or raped.

I wasn't stupid. I knew I couldn't help all children being abused or taken advantage of by becoming a social worker. But I could help some and I would fight with everything I had to make sure those children knew *they were worth something.* Those children needed to know life could get better and I would do anything in my power to make that happen for them.

So, for now I would hold onto that little spark inside of me for those children.

I would get the grades I needed and continue each day as it came.

I would do all that and then, finally, before I took any job with children, I would take the time to sort myself out. No past, no hurt, no pain of my own would reflect on any case I took on.

For now, I would continue to pray and hope that each day may be better than the last.

CHAPTER TWO

PICK

*L*ounging back on the couch in the compound while my brothers joked and laughed around me was nothing new. I enjoyed nights like that, just chilling and drinking. I never used to. After my brothers-in-arms found out I was double crossing the boss, my life had turned to shit.

For a while there, before I redeemed myself in Talon's eyes, in turn my brothers', I was glared at, smacked about, spat on and shouted at. All of it I could take, all of it was well deserved, and all of it was nothing compared to what my hellish life already had been. And *that* fucking said something.

What most of my biker brothers didn't know was how my life before Hawks had been a fucking nightmare.

My fucking mum was a bitch. Christ, bitch was too simple. She was true evil. From an early age, she was nothing but a bad dream. I was beaten, starved, and my body was sold so my mum could stay high or drunk.

What made my stomach churn, every fucking goddamn day, was the thought of not stopping her control sooner.

All I could think was that she was my mother, the one who birthed me. No matter how much shit she put me through, I should be there for her. She had no one else.

I wish I'd been smarter.

Guilt had the better of me for eight years. From when it all got worse at the age of twelve, when she started to sell my body to women *and men* for money. Which lasted for two years, until I had the physical strength to say no. However, those two years were what night terrors were made of. I had been touched, groped and taken in every way.

Fuck. Just thinking of it made bile rise in my throat. It made my body sweat and chest pound, even now twelve years later. I quickly took a pull of my beer, closed my eyes and leaned my head back against the couch.

Stupid motherfucking memories. I wished I could wipe them all out. I wished I could forget.

The only thing that eased any of it was...

No, I couldn't even go there, because then other memories would rise, even when they were good. When they were the cleanest and most precious ones I had in my sad fucking life.

Hell, they weren't even that momentous, but they made me smile. They made me feel.

Shit. I couldn't think of them because none of what I wanted, what kept the bad dreams at bay, would happen again.

She was gone.

And *he* didn't want anything to do with me.

Instead, my mind drifted back to the years after I stopped the selling of my body. When I took to stealing. The one bad thing about that was when I got caught and charged. Thank fuck I was only sixteen, so only had to do a small amount of time in juvie. The only good thing that came from stealing happened after I got out of juvie. In that small amount of time I was away, my stupid mum had racked up an even bigger debt. So I went back to stealing, which was what led me to Talon, my boss and my brother.

He'd caught me trying to knock off some of his tools in the Hawks' mechanical business off the compound. He beat me, but while doing it, he taught me a lesson. In the end, he gave me a job working on cars. It helped a fuckload with getting money in. Still, after a year, it wasn't enough. Mum was an addict. She no longer survived without her fix and if she didn't get it, she made my life hell. Christ, if it wasn't her making my life shit, it was her suppliers coming around taking stuff out on both of us.

Finally, at twenty-two I kicked the habit of supplying Mum with money after I saw my errors from that one night.

And after I risked my life for two gay guys.

How-fucking-ever, before that, I had fucked up big time by helping a bastard get his hands on Zara, Talon's woman. I'd let those pricks take her and the retribution I got in return for my fuck-up was earned. Having the crap beat out of me was nothing. I deserved more.

At least I was back in my brothers' good graces. I had proven myself in many ways with the help of Zara, Matthew and Julian. Fuck, not only them, but Zara's parents, and most of all Talon.

He was the one who knocked more sense into me. He was also the one to pay off all the debt my mum had. In return, I stopped all contact with her, which suited me just fucking fine.

Didn't stop her from trying though.

Not a week went by that I didn't hear her pleading messages about helping her out.

But no more.

I was done.

My life and my family were the brotherhood of Hawks.

For them, I would do anything. They had my respect and alliance.

My head straightened from the couch. I opened my eyes, because even over the music we all heard the front door to the compound slam shut behind someone. My brothers and I turned to the hall to see Talon's scowling, hard face stepped through, I knew something was wrong.

The whole room tensed.

Griz was the first to stand, then Blue.

My hand around the beer bottle tightened as Talon's

eyes searched the room. Fuck, when they landed on me, my heart pounded and I clenched my jaw. "Office, now," he ordered. I sent a chin lift and stood from the couch.

"Someone's gettin' another spanking. What you done this time, Pick?" Dodge asked.

Snorting, I replied with my middle finger and made my way down the hall that led to Talon's office. Opening the door, I found Griz and Blue already in there.

"Boss, what's goin' down?" I asked.

"Fuck," he hissed. A hand ran down his face as he stood stiff behind his desk. Griz sat on the couch in the corner and Blue leaned against the opposite wall, both were waiting for the shit news to be dealt. "Blue, go get Billy."

Now it was my body's turn to stiffen.

Billy the Kid. That was what he was named when he joined the Hawks MC because he was patched in as prospect at the age of fifteen. Now he was twenty-two. His real first name was Eli, last name Walker.

Eli Walker was... fuck, too much.

"Pick," Talon said to get my attention from the floor. They'd named me Pick because I was able to pick any lock. Nothing could stop me from getting in. My real name was Caden Adams. When my eyes met Talon's, he asked, "You okay?"

Obviously, I hadn't hidden my reaction of hearing Billy's name. Why I reacted was because I thought at one time Billy could mean something to me. I had been wrong, since then I hardly saw the guy. We steered clear of each other and that was fine by me. What also didn't help us was the fact we both loved the same woman.

Just as I sent a chin lift to boss-man, the door opened behind me. My hands fisted at my sides as Billy's heat appeared beside me.

"What's up?" Billy asked, his voice gruffer that usual. He didn't like that I was in the room. Well, tough fucking shit. I was over it all.

The next word from Talon had both Billy and my attention tenfold.

"Josie," he said, then stopped as if he wanted it to take affect and Christ, it did, because Josie was the woman we both loved. "Nancy rang me earlier. She wasn't herself, so I knew somethin' was up. Josie is havin' some trouble at school."

"What sorta trouble?" I asked through clenched teeth.

"Some dicks won't leave her alone. We all know what Josie is like. She hates any type of attention, especially from men."

"What's the plan, Boss?" Billy asked.

"I need the two of you to go to Melbourne, find out what the fuck is goin' on and fix it. No one causes shit for a Hawks family member. You hear me? Fix it good," Talon ordered.

"Done," I hissed.

Knowing someone was fucking with my woman caused my blood to boil. My ears rang from the sudden rush to the head. I wanted to find the fuckers and hurt them.

"Why the two of us?" Billy asked.

Closing my eyes for a second, I breathed deeply and opened them to the floor. He didn't want to work with me. Christ, I couldn't blame him. He knew what I wanted from him. He knew what he did to me and he knew my eyes followed him everywhere.

Only he didn't want any of it.

Instead of Talon answering the obvious, Griz did, "Josie trusts the two of you."

"She trusts you lot as well," I said.

"Maybe," Blue started. "But not like you two. She's more herself with the two of you, like she is with her parents and Wildcat. No one else will get the job done."

"And because of the way you both feel about her," Talon added.

Fuck. They all knew.

"Will you both be good boys and fix our girl's shit?" Talon asked with a smirk.

Bloody motherfucking hell. They'd all noticed things weren't right with Billy and me since Josie had left.

Billy and I... yeah, I had feelings for the kid, but he wouldn't let anything happen without Josie.

Josie was what made us stick.

Otherwise, Billy didn't want anything to do with a wanker like me. I had too much baggage. He'd found that out after the one night we'd shared together, after he'd sucked me off one drunken night and I'd become addicted to his touch.

Shit. Thinking of Billy's mouth around me was not a fucking good idea.

I was dirty. I was wrong in so many ways.

Wished I had time to go to the club, where I had no trouble getting sucked off or thrusting my cock into any pussy I wanted. It went either way at club Enchanted. If I wanted some random guy or woman, I could have either or both at the same time. But shit, I had no time for it. I was itching to get on the road, to deal with the dicks getting at Josie.

Letting our past go was what I had to do. Not thinking of Billy and Josie as my salvation was what I needed to focus on in order to fix Josie's problems and work as a team.

Then after, I could go back to being the sad sack of misery, waiting for my happily ever after like what my brothers had found.

"I'm fine," I growled.

"Yeah, Josie needs help. Once she's good, we'll come back."

"See if you can bring her back with you."

Griz scoffed. "She won't have it. She'll think she's a failure."

"Then we'll make sure she doesn't. She's my woman's sister, which means she's mine. She needs to be home with her family. She can study here in Ballarat where we can keep her safe."

"Deal," I said and walked toward the door, heading straight to my room.

Not having a house of my own, I lived in the compound. I liked it that way. It was easy for me to be there and help when shit went down.

Grabbing a bag out of the walk-in-closet, I started packing it with random clothes, my mind not really on it. Fury burned in my veins, my attention focused solely on Josie and the shit hand she'd been dealt once again.

Not for long though.

I knew Billy and I would do anything to stop her worries, make it right.

We'd risk anything... even our lives.

CHAPTER THREE

BILLY

*J*esus motherfucking Christ. Hearing Josie, the one woman who stole my heart, was in trouble, I wanted to slaughter everyone who did her wrong. Ever since I carried her small, scared body into the hospital four years ago, she owned me. Though, for two years I didn't let it show. Even though she was crushing on me, she'd been too young and messed up. Christ, she still was, and anyone who knew what had happened to her would understand why. I'd fought my feelings for her because she was sixteen and I was eighteen. But then, when she turned eighteen, I broke and told her I wanted her in my life. It was a lost cause because I wasn't the only one.

Caden "Pick" Adams also wanted her. He even had strong feelings for Josie Alexander. At the time, we thought we were doing the right thing by telling her how we felt, at the same time, we cared and wanted her to stay in Ballarat with us. To be with each of us to see who she would choose.

She was scared of the idea.

Frightened.

Both of us could see it swarming her eyes and making her body shiver.

So she chose no one.

Because she had been scared.

But most of all, it was because she didn't want to hurt either of us.

She couldn't see that she already had.

Josie was… Christ, she was everything. Sweet, shy, beautiful… everything.

Pick, hell, he was domineering and a pain. Most of all, he was fucking annoying because he was a good man. He was a man I needed to steer clear of to keep myself sane.

Not that I'd have much luck in the next month or so. Not until we'd clear Josie of her hell and we'd be apart once again.

Yeah, the next month or so was going to be hard for my sanity, body *and* heart.

As for why I stayed away from Pick for the last two years… I was a mean motherfucking biker. I wasn't some pining bi tool, wanting to suck another man's cock.

Crap. Scrap that cock thought from your head, idiot. It'll lead to dangerous thoughts.

Like the feel of Pick sliding his dick in and out of my mouth.

The taste of Pick on my tongue.

The way his body moved.

His face when he blew his load into my mouth.

And then after when he tried to... sleep beside me.

As if I meant something to him.

But I can't.

I won't.

Because Josie meant more to me than him.

Fucking hell.

Another lie, they both mean so much to me.

Was I even bi? I didn't know because there'd been only one man who had me thinking I could be. There'd been only one man I'd let touch me and sucked off. I had hoped it was the booze talking that night. I wasn't so sure anymore and hadn't been for a long time.

Confusion punctuated my every feeling and thought when it came to Caden Adams.

Christ, it was present with both him and Josie. I knew I wanted them both, but how could that possibly work? It was fucking weird. And I hated the thought if something did happen, our brothers would kick our arses for being strange motherfuckers.

I couldn't risk Josie or Caden. They'd been through enough shit in their lives..

Caden said he was bi. He knew he was because the night we were... together, he'd said he'd been to clubs. He'd had a taste of it and liked it.

That had made me jealous. Made me want to punch anything or anyone in sight.

I'd felt jealously about them both. Some days when I'd

see other brothers looking at Josie, as if they wanted a piece from her, I wanted to beat their fucking brains in. Never Caden though. I enjoyed seeing him watching her like I did, with so much emotion.

Still, with the two of them, I was cautious.

Because what punched me right in the gut, was the fact I knew about both of their pasts and both had been shit. So shit, I would do anything so nothing like that would happen again. Unfairness settled deep in my stomach as I packed my saddle bag. Why had two people who meant something to me—even when I was denying some of those feelings—had so much pain in their lives?

That injustice was also because my past had been nothing like theirs.

I was the rich kid in school. I was loved by my parents, even though they hated each other. Though by loved, I meant bought off with pricey shit. I wasn't beaten or raped. The only reason I joined Hawks MC was because I liked the fact women went crazy for a biker. I also needed a job. I didn't want my parents to think their money was all I needed from them. I wanted nothing from them really. They were cold, heartless bastards. So, at fourteen I took a job in Talon's garage. Cleaned, and worked on cars when a brother had the time to show me what to do. Learning wasn't hard. I was always a fast learner. In no time, I had my own customers and I was building my own Harley from scratch.

The only thing I never had was love.

That dumb fucking love feeling had me wishing I knew

Josie and Caden back then so I could have used my parents' money, the only time I would have taken it freely, to save them from their dangerous pasts.

That fucked-up love feeling had me thinking of Josie and Caden all the goddamn time.

Ride. That was what I needed to do. Get on my Harley and ride instead of thinking so fucking hard it hurt my head with a deep pounding behind my eyes.

Walking down the hall from my room at the compound, where I'd been living for four years, I rounded the corner and stopped at Caden's door.

Fuck. I had to remember to call him Pick.

I'd called him Caden that night, after he told me to.

Knocking, I heard a growled "enter", I opened the door to see him shouldering his bag. "You ready to roll?" I asked, staring at nothing but his face. Even when my eyes wanted to trace his body, I didn't let them.

Jesus, I needed to get laid. Pumping some pussy without anything on my mind but the sweet taste of an orgasm was what I needed.

"Yeah, let's get this over with."

Shit, all pussy thoughts left because Pick sounded like he didn't want to go at all, but I knew it'd be a lie. He'd do anything for Josie. Still, I found myself saying, "I can go on my fuckin' own if you prefer that?"

He glared at me, shouldered past me and walked out of the room. I followed, closing his door behind me.

Out at our Harleys, which were parked out the front of

the compound, I asked, "What's the plan? We goin' straight to Josie?"

After Pick had settled his bag to his bike, he swung a jean leg over and looked around at me as he shrugged into his leather jacket. "We find a place to stay. It'll be late by the time we get there, we'll wait 'til tomorrow. Catch Josie at school, then try and catch the fuckheads gettin' to her. After that, we deal with them."

Nodding, I said, "Sounds cool. Boss-man said we can stay at the compound in Caroline Springs."

He shook his head. "No, I want to stay close to the uni so we can get there early. I'm not sure of her schedule."

"I've got Nancy emailing it through to me," I said.

He sent a chin lift my way. "Good. Still, we're stayin' close. Now, let's move." He kick-started his Harley and it roared to life with no trouble at all. Quickly, I placed my helmet and gloves on. As soon as I had my bike going, Pick rolled out of the compound parking area and I followed behind.

The ride was over an hour and a half, and fuck it felt great. I hadn't had the chance for anything other than working in the boss' business. I'd happen to have a lot more customers recently, since goddamn Mindy Calhoun walked into the shop and liked what she saw in me. She was a fucking cougar. Even though she was hot for her age, there was no way I was sticking my dick in her. However, she'd sent all her cougar friends to the business and they'd all asked for me to service them. It was good for Talon's business, but not for me. Fucking loved my job, loved getting my hands on shit to fix. What I didn't love were the married whores who flirted, expecting to have a piece of my arse.

That was never going to happen.

Christ, I may look the part of their wet dreams, with my blond hair and blue eyes, but that was where it ended.

Still, they tried and when they did, it didn't fucking look good.

They'd wrap their bodies around me, touch me and fuck with me. When my brothers saw it, they all thought I was dipping into their snatches.

I swear even Pick thought it.

He'd seen it one day when Mindy had unexpectedly turned up. Pick walked in at the wrong time when Mindy had grabbed my hand and led it to her soaking panties under her short skirt. He soon walked straight back out, he hadn't seen me push her away.

Hell, I hadn't been with anyone in a fucking long time. My cock was aching for a sweet, tight hole, but all I gave it was my hand and images of two people.

Motherfucking Christ. I needed to change that. I needed to get laid or the next month or so was going to be harder than I imagined.

Shaking all thoughts from my head as we hit the city was best or else I'd end up as road kill and I couldn't have that, not when I had some shitheads to deal with.

Caden—*dammit*—Pick pulled up to a nice looking hotel. He slipped off his bike, pulled his helmet and gloves off and walked to the entrance. I wasn't far behind, so I heard him ask, "Two rooms."

The receptionist smiled seductively up at him. He was a tall fucker. I hated the way she licked her lips. "I'm sorry, sir, we only have one room available."

Of fucking course they did.

Shit.

His hands clenched at his sides. "There another hotel around?" he asked.

"Yes, but I presume they're all booked as well. There's a book signing going on at the moment. A lot of authors have travelled to Melbourne for it."

Fuck.

"Fine," Pick hissed through clenched teeth. "We'll take the room."

The bitch licked her lips again. "I, um, if your friend wants to stay in the room, I have a spare room for you at my house."

Jesus. It was my turn to clench my hands into fists so I didn't reach over the counter to slap the slut.

Pick's body tensed. "No. Just the room."

Take fuckin' that, you stupid whore.

She pouted. "I'm sure I could make your stay in Melbourne more... pleasurable."

Not being able to stop myself, I stepped up to the desk and growled, "Do you usually offer yourself up for customers? What would your boss think of that? I didn't know hookers were branching out and working day shifts in fuckin' hotels now."

She blanched, her once red cheeks turned ghostly white. "Right, one room. How long will you both be staying?"

"Don't know," Caden answered. I stepped back, glad he was the one to answer because I would have said something else she wouldn't like.

"It's one hundred and thirty a night." She smirked. The bitch changed her attitude and looked at us from head to toe, probably thinking we wouldn't be able to afford it.

"That's fine." Pick sighed.

"Great." She turned to get a paper that just printed out, and in that time, Pick looked over his shoulder at me. I glared. "Just sign here," the woman said. Pick did. "Thank you. You'll be in room 209, I hope you enjoy your stay," she said only to Caden.

In silence, we went out to our bikes, parked them in the underground car park of the hotel and took the lift to the fourth floor.

Once in the room, that held a small kitchenette and lounge, the room off to the side which no doubt held the bathroom in with it, I said, "I'll take the couch."

"Fine." His short reply pissed me off and when he walked off to the bedroom saying nothing else, I found myself furious.

Yeah. The month was going to be fucking hell.

CHAPTER FOUR

JOSIE

*M*y heart was in my throat. It was how I woke nearly every morning, with a sweaty, trembling body and my heart fighting its way out of my chest. Night terrors weren't a blast either. They were exhausting and terrifying. I had hoped over the last four years, since I was saved from David, the night terrors would eventually fade. They hadn't.

What helped them stay, my guess, was because I was weak.

It was also the fact that my life was upside down once again.

"Josie, time to get your cute butt moving," Simone yelled from the hall. She would be walking past so she could get to the bathroom first, which was why I started taking showers at night; she took too long in the bathroom, making us both late.

Even though I had just woken with fright filling my veins, I smiled.

I smiled because Simone could do that to a person. That smile may not reach my eyes, but it helped me get out of bed each morning. It also helped me continue each day to reach the goals I wanted to.

Climbing out of bed, I donned a pair of jeans and a flannel shirt. It was big, but warm on the colder days in winter. Packing my bag, my mind drifted to my family in Ballarat. I wondered what they were all doing. Would Zara already be up with her twins who were turning three in a couple of months? Would Julian and Mattie's plans for their wedding be all organised?

My thoughts even glided to Deanna, or Hell Mouth as most called her. It was only just over a year ago she had her baby boy, Nicholas. Zara had emailed me a video recorded by Dodge. I'd lost count of the amount of times I'd watched it. Still, every time had me laughing and smiling, then wishing I was home.

"Are you recording?" Zara asked, smiling into the camera.

"Is the fuckin' light flashing red, Wildcat?" Dodge growled.

"Yes."

"Then it's recordin'."

"Awesome." Zara smiled and started walking down a hall. "Hey, Josie, I wish you were here today. We miss you so much. However, seems you're working hard studying, so I thought I'd share this special day with you this way." She stopped, faced the

camera, and clapped with glee. "Guess what, Deanna is having her baby right now." She turned and then rounded the corner. The camera adjusted to zoom in on Deanna standing at the bar, one hand supporting herself on the wooden top while her body bent forward as she breathed hard.

Her head turned toward the camera, her eyes widening. "What in the fuck are you doing?"

"I've got Dodge to film it for Josie," Zara said.

"Are you fucking high?" Deanna bellowed and then all thoughts flew from her mind when a contraction started. She moaned in pain. Griz stepped up behind her to rub her back.

"We need to get to the hospital," he growled.

"Shit, shit, shit," Deanna chanted. Her head turned to a smiling Zara and glared. "How in the fuck did you do this twice? You're fucking crazy to want to go through it again. Crazy, stupid w-w-woman. Jesus," she screamed. Zara wasn't crazy. She was the nicest person I knew, I was so proud to call her my sister. What she was doing for Julian and our brother, Mattie, was amazing. Willing to give them a gift of having their own child... My sister was wonderful.

"Car's ready. Let's roll," I heard Talon's voice coming from somewhere off camera.

"This is where I hand it over to you, boss. I ain't coming to the hospital," Dodge said from behind the camera as it filmed Griz helping Deanna walk toward the hall to the front door.

"You promised my woman to do it, you're fuckin' doin' it," *Talon ordered.*

"Fuck," Dodge snapped.

"What the fuck are you looking at?" Deanna yelled at someone

off camera. Only then her hand whipped out taking hold of some material.

"Princess, let Dive go."

"You all should be in pain if I am," Deanna yelled to the room. "You all need to suffer."

"Believe me, we are," Dodge uttered. Deanna turned to him. "Shit," he hissed.

"Deanna, we're gettin' to the motherfuckin' hospital before you pop our kid out right here on the floor. Now move."

"It isn't the cleanest place," Zara offered.

Griz glared at Zara and with Talon's help, they moved Deanna out of the compound and into the car. Dodge, with the camera, climbed into the back of Griz's four-wheel drive while Talon hopped in behind the wheel. Zara climbed into the passenger seat leaving Deanna and Griz to the back seat. Dodge leaned over the back seat to film Deanna resting her head on Griz's legs. He ran his hand through her hair. I was lucky enough to see her soft smile.

The camera jolted around as the car moved. With Talon driving, I knew he would be swerving through traffic.

"I'm going to hurt you for this," Deanna groaned, looking up at her man. Her hand came up and gripped his tee.

"I look forward to it, princess." Griz chuckled.

"Zara," Deanna screamed. "Oh, fuck, I feel like I want to push."

"Oh, God," Zara gasped.

"What?" Griz yelled.

"It means she's close."

"Kitten, will we make it to the hospital?"

"I need to push," Deanna screamed. "Grady, you fucker, oh, God, I don't want our kid born in our car."

"It'll be okay." He nodded down at her. "Wildcat?" he asked in a panicked voice, a voice I had never heard from him before.

With wide eyes, Zara ordered, "Talon, pull over. Call an ambulance." Once he did, she climbed out of the car, must have run around to Deanna's side, because the door was flung open. "I need to take your panties off," Zara said, her hands sliding up under Deanna's skirt.

"Hot damn, girl action," Dodge foolishly said.

The camera was then dropped and all I heard were voices.

"Shut the fuck up," Griz growled. "Get out, get out now before I kill you."

"Zara," Deanna screamed.

"She's crowning, the baby's coming," Zara yelled. "Push, Dee, push."

"Come on, princess, you can do this."

"Of... fucking... course... I... can," Deanna bellowed.

In the next second, a baby's cry was heard and my heart melted.

The video ended in the hospital, capturing Deanna, the hardest woman I knew, smiling sweetly down at her baby boy, with Griz standing protectively over them.

"Jose, come on girlfriend," Simone yelled. I opened my door and walked down the hall to see her waiting at the front door.

"Sorry," I said and picked up my backpack from the floor just as we heard a door behind us open. Parker, looking sleep deprived, walked out of his room in nothing but boxers. I heard Simone sigh in appreciation. I would have also, but I quickly bit my bottom lip. He staggered his way to the bathroom at the end of the hall without a hello or anything.

"Damn, that man is fine," Simone whispered. I gave her a tight-lipped smile and a small nod before I opened our front door and walked out. She was right though. Parker was fine. His body seemed as though it were etched from stone: hard and beautiful.

However, he was a mystery and I wasn't sure what his life was like or if I wanted to know anything about it.

It happened early that morning. Simone and I had gone to our class. During it, there was only one of Cameron's friends taunting me. Coughing out harsh names and poking me in the back with his pen. Simone turned and glared at the guy, but she didn't see the jabs, thank goodness, or else she would have made a scene. When the bell rang, knowing Simone had a class at the opposite end of the building, I quickly said goodbye and bolted from the room.

The frigid air swirled around me, causing me to shiver as I rushed along the pathway to the building that held my next class. I gripped my backpack tighter in my arms against my stomach, wishing I had brought a jacket with me.

Unfortunately, I didn't make it far before I felt someone

behind me. My already hasty pace picked up another notch. Something brushed my back.

Please no.

Just leave me alone.

However, no matter the amount of inner begging I did, I knew I was out of luck when next my hair was tugged back violently, causing my steps to falter and I cried out in pain.

After righting myself, I turned around to face my assailant, only to cringe when a hand was wound around my waist. I tried to step away, but it tightened.

"Come on, girl. I know you said no to Cameron, but you'd be willing for me, yeah?"

Dropping my bag, I raised my hands and pushed against Scott's chest. Scott was nearly as bad as Cameron, which could explain why they were best friends.

"Leave me alone," I said, raising my glare to meet his eyes, then I cursed my lips as they trembled.

He chuckled. "I can't do that. I've always wanted what Cameron wants and I plan to get it this time." Two guys behind him laughed. When had they arrived?

It was then my heart seized in my chest as soon as I heard a certain noise.

My already tense body froze solid.

My eyes widened.

Was it?

Could it be?

Family?

"What...?" Scott said.

Blinking rapidly, I looked around everywhere to find

that noise as I pushed harder against Scott's chest. He started saying something to me, but my ears and eyes weren't for him... no, they were for the two Harleys riding through the campus car park and coming to a stop just at the edge of the lawn.

My struggle continued. Couldn't Scott see my attention wasn't on him? Couldn't he and his friends sense the trouble they would be in, depending on who was on those two bikes?

Suddenly, Scott must have noticed others around us looking toward the new arrivals. Scott stood straight, and I saw out the corner of my eyes as he gestured to his friends to the two men hopping off their bikes. Scott's arm fell from my waist. I sagged in relief and drew in a deep breath. Only Scott's hand quickly and tightly gripped my wrist.

It seemed he wasn't willing to let me go as we all watched the two Harley riders unclasp their helmets, remove their sunglasses and place both on their seats. When they turned back to face me, I gasped.

Home.

Family.

Love.

Safety.

My free, trembling hand came up to my mouth to cover it as Caden and Eli stalked their way toward us. They both looked amazing, but also very unhappy. Caden dug a baseball cap out of the back pocket of his jeans and placed it on his head backwards. He seemed somewhat calmer than Eli, who was rolling his head side to side, also clenching and unclenching his hands.

They stopped just a foot in front of us. Caden's gruff voice barked out, "You wanna let go of her." It wasn't a question. Every syllable was a demand, but Scott wasn't smart enough to know that.

"Nope. You wanna fuck off and mind your own business?"

Caden's eyes hardened. His gaze travelled to Scott's hand around my wrist. Slowly, he pulled his glare back up to me, and his eyes softened.

"Caden," I uttered, my gaze flicked to the fuming man next to him. "Eli," I whispered. Eli's eyes touched mine briefly only to move back to Scott's quiet friends watching the whole scene apprehensively. Eli was in the zone. That wasn't good.

My eyes went to Caden, only his focus was back on Scott. He sighed and then snorted. "You don't know it, but you'll soon get it. She is ours—"

Scott burst out laughing. He tugged on my wrist so I was looking at him. "So you don't hold out for everyone? Knew you were a slut."

"Pick," Eli growled, using Caden's biker name.

"Not yet, Billy," Caden ordered. I'd always liked Eli's biker name, Billy the Kid.

Caden took a step closer. "You really need to get it and fuckin' soon. Josie Alexander is ours, as in, she *is* fuckin' family. She *is* Hawks. Do you understand that, dickhead?"

In frustration, Scott's hand gripped harder. I flinched

from the pain and Caden saw it. Before I knew it, Caden had his hand around Scott's throat. My wrist was instantly free because Caden was pushing Scott backward, so far back he collided with the building and shrubbery surrounded their legs.

Worry settled deep. Worry they would soon be in trouble because of me.

There was so much to take in. Gasps, squeals and screams sounded around me.

Eli punched one of Scott's mates and then the other. He dodged the fists flying his way and landed a hit to one of the guys' stomach, causing him to double over. Eli went straight for the other and in seconds, after two jabs, the guy was on the ground.

Tense silence filled the air and then…

"This is your last chance, fucker. You go near Josie again, your life will fuckin' end. She is a part of Hawks Motorcycle Club. You want to fuckin' continue givin' her shit, then payback—*major goddamn payback*—where your life will be not worth livin' will come your way. Do. You. Get. Me?" Caden growled so close into Scott's face.

My head swung to Eli when he hissed out, "Move again and I will stab the fuck outta you." To prove his point, he took a switch blade out of the back of his jeans and flipped it open.

"Eyes to me, cockhead," Caden snapped at Scott.

Doors near us were banged open. Three lecturers ran through them and toward our way.

"Caden, please," I begged.

"Right. Last warning, go near her, look at her, or touch her, your life is mine." With that, he pulled back his fist and punched Scott in the stomach and then stepped back as Scott crumbled over with his arms folded around his middle.

"Hey," a lecturer yelled.

Without a thought, I made a step to Eli, who was the closest, reaching out a hand to touch his arm. He saw me coming, but my courage blinked out and my hand fell to my side. "You both have to go. I don't want you in trouble. Please."

"Precious," Caden said first, my eyes went to him to see him smile. "Don't worry about us."

"What is the meaning of this?" Lee Eden demanded. He was one of my lecturers, the class I was supposed to be attending.

"Nothin' at all. We just popped in to see our friend, Josie," Eli said. My eyes ran over his body to see the switch blade he had held was no longer in sight.

Eden raised his bushy brows. He looked to the other two members of staff, ones I didn't know. One shrugged and the other shook his head.

"Scott? Anything to add?"

Scott, with a scowl upon his face, stood tall and shook his head. "Nothing."

A lecturer scoffed. "We saw the assault with our own eyes. Do you want to press charges?"

My heart stopped.

Caden snorted. "What you saw was me helping Scott. He

was choking. I thought a tap to the stomach would help bring up whatever was stuck." With a sweeping hand, Caden gestured to Scott. "And would you look at that, he's fine now."

"Scott?" Eden pressed.

"All good."

"Fine. If you have class, best you get going." With one final glare, he turned with the other staff members and walked off.

"Your warning has been noted," Scott started and then smiled. "But good luck getting Cameron to listen." A friend of his tugged on his arm. Scott looked over his shoulder at him and nodded. "Looks like we'll get some entertainment over the next week or so," he finished, then walked off with his friends following.

For the first time, my heart settled, and I drew in a deep breath. Slowly, my eyes moved back to the two men in front of me. Through hooded eyes I studied them. Caden wore jeans, a tank top, with his biker cut over it, and a backward baseball cap. Eli was dressed similar, only he wore a tee but with no cut over it.

"Precious," Caden uttered. My heart jumped when his arms went wide. I shuffled forward and slowly touched my hands to his waist, next my forehead went to his chest. Both men were taller than I was.

Breathing deeply, taking in what consumed my thoughts every day, I wrapped my arms around his waist. His own arms settled down at his sides. He knew, more than anyone,

I wasn't in the right frame of mind to be touched. Too much had just happened. My senses were already haywire.

"Baby," he whispered into my hair and ran his chin on the top of my head. My breath hitched.

Caden was here.

Eli was here.

With a final intake of all that was Caden—leather and warming spices—I turned from his arms and directly into Eli's, who was waiting for me. Eli, knowing me also, rested his arms at his sides as I took from him the comfort I needed. Only these two men could I touch freely. From the whispered voices around us, maybe my unwanted attention or touching hadn't gone unnoticed like I thought it had, then again maybe they were just admiring my men. My home.

"Sweetheart," Eli said with a smile in his voice. I rubbed my cheek against his chest in answer, because I wasn't ready to move or talk. His lips touched the back of my neck. I stiffened for only a second, breathing in Eli's scent of his Prada Luna cologne helped my mind to know I wasn't in danger. I was being taken care of.

Stepping away, I asked, "What are you both doing here?"

"Just visitin', precious, and I'm glad we did. Who was that wanker?"

Shrugging, I looked to the ground and said, "Just an annoying someone."

"Sweetheart, you wanna tell us what's goin' on and who Cameron is?" Eli asked.

"Maybe we should go somewhere first?" Caden suggested.

Nodding, because so many eyes were still on us, I thought it would be wise to get away from uni to somewhere more private. Not that I was sure I was going to tell them everything that had been happening. If I did, Cameron may only live until the morning. Not that it would be a loss, but I didn't want Caden or Eli arrested for anything, especially an idiot like Cameron.

"We can go back to my place," I said and grabbed my mobile from my back pocket. All thoughts of returning to class left my mind. "I just have to let Simone know where I'll be."

"Who's she?" Eli asked.

A stab of jealously gutted me. I didn't like Eli asking, but I had no right over him or Caden. I had pushed them both away because I couldn't pick between either of them and that situation hadn't changed.

Clearing my thick throat, I answered, "A friend I live with. She's been... everything since I came here."

"We must thank her." Eli smiled.

And how will you do that? I found myself snapping.

Good God. I needed to control myself. I had never had the urge to snap at anyone, no matter the situation. However, I found myself wanting to do anything and everything so Eli and Caden didn't... what? Sway to someone else?

What was wrong with me?

Was it because I had missed them so much?

Because they reminded me of home?

No, they are my home.

Both of them?

How could I think that?

"Precious, you look exhausted. Let's get you home." Upon my nod, Caden picked up my forgotten backpack from the ground and steered me toward his Harley. After loading my items in his saddle bag, he asked where I lived. Thankfully, it wasn't far from school.

Once I informed him, he straddled his seat and patted the space behind him. If it were anyone else, I wouldn't have climbed on. But being Caden, or even if it were Eli, they both knew what I was comfortable with. So, as soon as I was seated, I placed my arms at his waist when he fired up his beauty. Finally, a smile lit my face as we pulled out of the park and rode off. It had been too long, too long since I was on a bike, and too long since I felt safe, surrounded in warmth from the two most important men in my life.

CHAPTER FIVE

JOSIE

J had forgotten Parker was home, so when I silently led Caden and Eli into our apartment, I let out a startled gasp when my eyes landed on Parker casually sitting on the lounge chair watching the television. Only I wished I had kept my mouth shut tight, because in the next second, I was moved out of the way, behind the frame of Eli and into the arms of Caden, while Eli took out his pistol and pointed it at Parker.

"Who in the fuck are you?" Eli demanded.

As if he were bored, Parker raised one brow and looked calmly back at Eli, as if having a gun pointed at him was the norm. "I could ask the same question." He glanced over Eli's shoulder to meet my shocked gaze. "You bringin' trouble around here again, woman?"

"Don't fuckin' look at her," Eli barked.

Parker rolled his eyes and stood.

"Eli," I uttered. "Please."

Eli took in my tone, a tone that told him he was in the wrong and stood straight, lowering his gun. I puffed out a stressed breath.

What else would the day scare me with?

"Name's Parker. I own this place and live here when I'm not working. Now what has the little girl brought home with her?"

Little girl?

Caden's hands, which I hadn't noticed, fell from my shoulders as he stepped around me. "Name's Pick, this is Billy. We ride with Hawks MC and heard Josie had some trouble. We're here to fix it."

They'd heard?

How?

I watched as Parker actually smirked. "Good to see someone has her back." He looked to me and asked, "How'd someone like you get involved with an MC?"

Eli chose to answer for me. "She's our prez's sister-in-law."

Parker raised his brow again. "So many things I don't know about you, kid."

With a tight smile, I shrugged. "I could say the same for you, Parker."

He laughed. "That you could."

"Why haven't you helped Josie before?" Eli asked in a rough tone.

"Eli," I scolded.

"No, it's all good. I'm not around much. When that dick came here, I helped get rid of him, but I'm not her babysitter. I couldn't follow her around, and even if I wanted to, I had shit to deal with myself."

"Parker, I would never expect you—"

"Honey, it killed me to see the pain in your eyes. I wanted to help. I wanted to follow you and beat the shit out of anyone who did you wrong. But I was hardly here and when I wasn't here, it ate me up inside thinkin' of the crap you were going through. You're a beautiful star, Josie, you don't deserve any of it."

Goodness gracious.

It was the most I had heard Parker talk and what he'd said blew me away. Never would I have thought Parker thought of me while he was away.

Looking to the floor with heated cheeks, I said, "You did help. You kept our home safe for me to be myself. For me to have a place I could feel protected in and for that, I thank you."

"No need for thanks, kid." Looking up, I saw a smirk on his face. "I see I lost a chance that I never really had, but wanted."

Biting my bottom lip, my hand went to my chest as my heart beat hard behind it.

What was he saying?

"You two had better take care of her where I couldn't," Parker said. With my eyes wide, he walked up to me. Caden and Eli tensed. "You deserve happiness, honey. I hope you find it." My body stilled when he raised a hand and gently ran his fingers across my cheek.

"Back off," Caden growled.

Parker laughed. "Yeah, yeah. I know a claim when I see one... " he looked from my eyes to Caden, then Eli, "or two." He shook his head and finished with, "I'll be seeing you, kid. Or not. I've got to head out of town." He stepped back, and it was then I noticed his bag by the front door as he made his way to it.

"Parker," I called. He turned. "Um, take care."

He sent me a wink and a smile before walking out of the apartment.

It was obvious the day wasn't over with surprises.

"I don't like that guy." Eli sighed. Caden nodded in agreement. I quickly bit my bottom lip to hide my smile and headed to the kitchen beside the living area. Our apartment was bigger than most in Melbourne, holding three bedrooms, one bathroom, a living room and separate kitchen. The laundry room was shared between the other three apartments and situated down in the basement. I loved living there. The apartment, even being owned by a man, had an appealing décor. The walls were a soft yellow. The furniture was mostly wooden and seemed handmade instead of store bought. It was peaceful.

"Would anyone like a coffee?" I asked, heading straight for the kettle. I knew I needed one. Hopefully, it would help me stay alert.

"Thanks, precious," Caden said as he sat at the small four-seated table.

"Love one, sweetheart." Eli smiled, also sitting down, only he turned his chair backward to straddle it.

"Good, then you can both explain how you heard about my troubles and why you both came... not just for a visit, I'm presuming."

As I fluttered around preparing our drinks, I caught the eye roll from Eli and a smirk from Caden, which they gave each other.

They would soon find out that in the last two years, I'd grown somewhat of a backbone... only those who were important in my life would probably tell. I still, of course, had trouble with people I hardly knew. Trust was something to earn and was not freely given. The two men at the table I trusted deeply, with my very soul. They would get to see how I had grown into a woman.

Turning from the bench, I set their coffees in front of them and then claimed my own chair between both of theirs. Raising my eyebrows, I waited.

Caden scoffed. "All right, precious. All we know is that somehow Talon found out that you were having some troubles from people at school. He asked us to come here and check it out, see if we could help."

Eli leaned into the chair more to catch my eye. "What I want to know is why you thought you'd deal with this on your own in the first place, Josie?"

"Billy," Caden growled.

"No," Eli barked. He stood from the chair and paced the small space behind the table. "You have people who care about you, sweetheart. You don't have to deal with shit, fuckin' pathetic crap, being dished out by some fuckin' loser." He stopped and turned to me. "All you had to do was call. Why didn't you? Shit, how long have you been dealing with it all on your own?" He stood above me with his hands balled into fists. He didn't like what I'd been going through. He didn't like the thought of me on my own.

Slowly, I reached out and wound my hand around his fist. Shock registered on his face, his eyes flaring and then, once they settled, he unwound his fist and entwined our fingers.

I smiled up at him before my gaze went to Caden. My arm slid onto the table. I held my hand palm up for Caden's. He didn't hesitate, he also seemed surprised by my willingness to want to touch them. Silly men, didn't they know they were my home. They were what helped keep me going. At school, it had been too soon for them to touch me, especially after being held violently against Scott's body. However, now I was in my home, it was on my terms. I knew they wouldn't push me for more than what I was willing to give.

"It was stupid of me really. I wanted to prove I could do this... I guess more to myself than anything or anyone else. I wanted to know I could live out in the real, tough world on my own, without my security blanket, my family who'd go above and beyond to protect me. I-I still want that... but, I know now that what I want above everything, and *is* more important than anything. I want my family."

"You want to go home to Ballarat?" Caden asked.

"Yes. Only not yet. I have four months left before school

ends for the year. I do have the opportunity to transfer my degree to an open university course, so I can study from home. But then… yes, then I want to come home to Ballarat."

"You know we won't leave you with that dickhead still harassing you," Eli stated.

Smiling sadly, I said, "I can't have you both here for that long. You both have lives of your own. I won't ask you to put that on hold and stay to be… my bodyguards for that amount of time. I could ring Talon and ask him to send a prospect. Then at least Talon won't be losing two valuable employees and members."

"I'll talk to Talon about it," Caden said.

"Pick," Eli barked.

A meaningful look passed between them and Caden once again said, "I'll talk to Talon about it." Eli then nodded and sat back down at the table without letting go of my hand. "But first, our girl needs to call home."

"What?" I whispered.

"Precious, your parents are worried about you. Call them," Caden said, sliding his phone over the table. I stared down at it. When I didn't reach for it, he picked it back up and pressed some buttons. He placed it back on the table and it started ringing.

"Hello?" my mum's voice said.

"Nance, Pick here with Eli *and Josie*."

"Darling?" Mum's uttered, her voice catching.

"Hi, Mum. I'm so sorry for worrying you. I promise I won't do it again."

"Oh, Lordy, my son-in-law is a miracle worker and sending two handsome men. Amazing. Sweetie, how are you?"

"I'm good now, Mum." I smiled at the phone.

In the background we heard boomed, "Is that Josie? Give me the phone, woman." There was a shuffle and then Dad's voice was on the line. "Baby girl, is this actually our daughter who we haven't heard from in a long time?"

Giggling, I said, "Yes, Dad. Caden and Eli are here also."

"Who?" he snapped.

Rolling my eyes, I said, "Pick and Billy."

"Yo, Rich." Caden said.

"S'up, Rich." Eli smiled.

"You boys there to take care of our baby girl?"

"Course," Caden said.

"You boys gonna keep your hands to yourself?" Dad demanded as we heard in the background from Mum, "I hope they don't." Dad covered the phone and said something to Mum and then into the phone, "Well?"

"We'll try, Rich." Eli smirked and winked at me while my cheeks heated.

Silence on the other end.

Then, "Well, shit, at least you're being honest. You know what will happen if you screw her over."

"Dad, I'm still here."

"Quiet, Josie. The big guys are talkin'."

"Mum," I called loudly.

"Richard, give me the phone," Mum snapped.

"No, I'm talking to the guys. They need to know they'll

be effed up if they cause our daughter any harm, even to the heart."

"Don't be stupid. They've been in love with her since she was seventeen."

Goodness me.

Was that true?

Looking to the guys to see their reactions, they'd both adverted their gazes from mine and kept blank expressions, so I couldn't tell.

Still, the phone call was just getting strange. It was time to end it. "Mum, Dad, we have to go. Um, I love you both and I promise to talk soon."

"Love you, sweetie. Take care and make sure you practise safe sex."

Heck it to hell.

"Shut up, Nancy. Love you, too, baby girl, but do not listen to your mother. Sex leads to a huge amount of trouble. Look at me, I married mine."

"Richard!" Mum snapped before the call disconnected.

Sighing, I slid the phone back to Caden. "That was… *very* awkward."

"Remind me to leave the phone call off speaker and just for you to deal with them," Caden said with a nod.

We all heard the front door open. Eli was standing in seconds. His hand going to the back of his pants.

"Josie?"

I reached out to Eli, laying my hand on his arm. "It's just Simone, my friend and housemate."

Who was beautiful. Would the guys notice? Would they want... her?

She came striding into the kitchen and halted in the doorway. "Um... hi."

A giggle escaped me to see the shock on her face. Her mouth actually dropped open. "Simmy, this is Caden and Eli," I explained.

"Hey," Caden said with a smile.

Eli sent her a chin lift before sitting back down.

"They're *your* Caden and Eli...? Holy shit, woman. You've been holding out on me."

A blush crept onto my cheeks and then deepened when Eli teased, "*Your* Eli and Caden, sweetheart?"

Simone scoffed. "Ah, yeah, she talks about you two all the time."

Let me die right now.

I wanted to hide my face, but I didn't, and I was glad because then I would have missed the look, a look I didn't understand passed between Eli and Caden.

What did *that* mean?

"Now I know why you left uni early, Josie. Totally understandable to leave for your guys' visit. You two staying long?" Simone asked as she sat at the only spare seat left at the table.

"Not sure yet, have to speak to Talon." Caden smiled.

Simone paused to take notice of that smile, like many women would. "Josie's brother-in-law, right?"

"Yep."

"Cool. While you're here, you guys going to deal with the jackarse?"

"Simone." I glared.

"We've already dealt with one named Scott, that him?" Eli asked after taking a sip of his coffee.

"That's one, but not the major dickhead."

"Simone," I snapped.

"What?" She raised her hands in the air and then thumped them back on the table. "They need to know. It's why they're here, why I spoke with… " She sat back and slid down in her seat a little, whispering, "Shit."

I gasped. "*You* told my mum?"

She shook her head. "Not really."

"Nancy rang your phone. You didn't pick up, Simone did. Nancy rang Talon and then asked us to come. We were more than willing, precious. No one fucks with Hawks, babe. You know this," Caden said.

Simone told my mum everything, my foster mum, my only mum really. That explained what Mum had said before. Part of me was hurt and annoyed that Simone went behind my back. Betrayed even. I knew she saw that written on my face as she looked at me. Her stare turned apologetic. She mouthed *sorry*.

Ashamed was also high on my list of things to feel. I was ashamed that I didn't put a stop to it all in the first place. God, it took my friend to open up to *my* family on my behalf. It should have been me. Instead, I was being stubborn, thinking I could deal with it all on my own. The tears I shed nearly every day should have told me to pull up my big girl panties and seek help. My family had always wanted to be there for me. I knew that, yet I kept them away... for what? Nothing.

At least they were with me now. They had my back. I had their trust and love.

"I'm sorry," I said to Simone. "I'm sorry I wasn't the one who reached out for help from my family. I'm sorry it took you to do it. Most of all, I'm sorry for having you worry about me when I should have dealt with it."

She reached across the table for my hand. It was fast, so I flinched, only she ignored it and took hold. "You weren't in the right head space, honey. I know you wanted to try and deal with it all on your own, but I couldn't stand seeing you lose yourself more and more each day. I wasn't enough to keep you afloat. I knew you needed more, you needed your family."

Tears shined in my eyes. "It was cruel of me to put you through that. But Simone, you helped to keep me going each day. You helped me in many ways and seeing Caden and Eli today... the tightness in my chest has eased. Having people who are a part of my family here already feels wonderful and it makes me feel safe. Still, you have to know, honey, you are a part of my family as well."

Her smile turned bright. "You know I love ya, honey." She looked to both men and cleared her throat. "But we're probably getting too emotional for these badarse bikers." She stood from her chair, her hand falling from mine. "Where are you two staying? I could always share my bed."

"Simone!" I scolded.

She laughed. "I'm teasing, Josie. I know these two are yours... unless you're willing to share...?" I was about to snap again when she held her hand up in front of her. "Teasing. Well, somewhat. Anyway, I'm heading for a shower. You three have a nice chat now." With a final appreciative look to Eli and Caden, she walked out of the room.

"Sweetheart," Eli started. Once my gaze and red cheeks met his, he continued, "I think you have some explainin' to do on just what you've told your friend about us."

"I-um, I. You see... " The truth echoed loud and clear in my heart. *It was only that I couldn't stop thinking about you both, and the situation, when you both came to me asking me to pick between the two of you, but I couldn't. And now I find myself wishing I had both of you to love and both of you to myself.* However, there was no way I could choose between the man who carried me away from my disaster of a life and the man who swooped in and took down my defences. Both of them meant so much to me. Both of them held a part of my heart. To hurt one, by picking the other, was inconceivable.

Which was also why I should turn them away. I should call Talon myself and ask for someone else's help, because having the two of them there, so close to me, would make it harder for me to stay away from them.

Never had I thought I would feel desire to be with another person again after what I lived through with David. Never had I thought my mind would imagine what it would be like to... see them naked, to see what their hands, mouths and bodies could do to me.

Goodness, even thinking of it caused my panties to become damp.

Though, no matter how turned on I could be from thoughts of them both, I was still scared. I didn't know if David had ruined me for anyone else. I didn't know if I could enjoy the time in bed with a man. I never liked it when David touched me, when he was inside of me. Never once did I enjoy it. I couldn't help but worry that it meant there was something wrong with me down there.

I also worried that when, or if, the time came, I would freak out. What would happen if I started having a panic attack while being intimate with someone? Could that person understand why I was so freaked and stop? Or would they be selfish, which was how I only knew men could be in the bedroom.

Then again, I knew nothing much about men.

What I did know wasn't really worth a mention, because my only knowledge came from a man who haunted my dreams. A man who was brutal, mean and rough.

"Precious," Caden's soft voice broke through my thoughts. "Where is your mind at right now?"

Shrugging, I replied quietly, "Many places really."

"Josie, you know you don't need to be scared with us," Caden said.

My brows shot up. "What do you mean?"

"It's okay to have been thinking about us. It's okay that you've spoken to Simone about us. You've been on our minds as well."

"I-I have?"

Eli snorted. "Hell, sweetheart, there ain't a day goes by that I don't think about you. I'm sure it's the same with Pick."

My heart bloomed. Did that mean they still cared for me that way?

Still, there was the problem of having to choose between the two of them.

"Have you ever…?" Eli started. I looked to him to see his cheeks held a tinge of red. I bit my bottom lip to keep from laughing at this biker man getting embarrassed about something. He cleared his throat. "Have you ever been with anyone other than that fuckhead?"

Now I understood why he'd been embarrassed, because now I was as well.

"I, oh, heck. Um." Instead of answering, I shook my head, my gaze to my lap. I couldn't believe we were talking about it already. It seemed two years should have severed our connection, but having them there, it was obvious it hadn't. They still felt they could ask or say anything that was on their minds to me.

"Billy," Caden growled.

"Shit, sorry." Eli sighed.

Caden obviously knew it was too soon to be talking about such things. Which left Eli probably feeling as though he'd done something terrible for even bringing it up. I didn't want him to feel that way. I would like to talk to them both about it, only just not yet. I didn't know where it was all going. I didn't know if they were staying or if I still had to pick between them. Goodness, I didn't even know what I was thinking.

I couldn't think that.

Having them both.

It wasn't right.

Still, the thought of it, of having the two men who had stolen my heart many years ago, caused my heart to race and my lady parts to quiver.

Suddenly, I stood. "I um, I have to get ready for work."

Caden nodded. "We're gonna quickly grab some things and make some calls. We'll see you at your work. Are you okay getting there?"

After nodding, I started for the doorway, only to stop and look over my shoulder. "Eli," I called and he looked over at me. "I don't mind you asking. I would like... one day, to talk about these things. I guess, I'm just shy and still confused."

"Confused about what, sweetheart?"

Was I really going to say it? "Confused about the way you both make my body want to feel again." Yes, I was. With that, I left two stunned bikers in the kitchen.

CHAPTER SIX

PICK

*W*e made it outside before I said anything, and from the look on Billy's face, he was just as surprised about Josie's comment as me. Never had I thought our girl, our shy, timid girl would turn into a minx. Christ, my cock immensely enjoyed the fact that I made her want to feel again. From the look in her eyes, it told me she was feeling more than just friendship. Lust had been present when those words flew from her mouth. "Two years and it's like I'm learning about Josie all over again," I said.

Nodding, Billy grinned. "Tell me about it." He snorted. "I thought I fucked up royally, but then she blew me away with what *she* said."

"She's attracted to us both," I stated the obvious. She

would have said one of us made her body feel things, but she hadn't. She'd said both of us.

"I know."

"What are we gonna do? I don't want to scare her, and I don't want her to... be hurt in any way."

"Having her pick between us would hurt her."

Looking down at the road, I thought over our options. My gaze went to Billy as he was gettin' on his helmet.

"We headin' to the hotel?" he asked.

"Yep." I went to my own ride and put my shit on. "Billy," I called.

"Yeah?" he answered, sliding his leg over his Harley.

"On the way there, I want you to think about somethin'." After he gave me a chin lift to say he was listening, I continued, "I need to know if you'd be willing to share Josie's affection."

Before he could say anything, I swung my leg over my girl, placed my helmet on and kicked her into gear, riding straight out and heading to the hotel.

Fuck. I hoped he'd consider sharing Josie. I was sick of the time we'd already wasted and now I knew she had feelings for the both of us, there was no more time to waste. I was willing to spread the time among the three of us if it meant Josie would be my woman in one way or another.

Billy was the only other man I was willing to share with and that was because I knew what he felt for Josie was as strong as how I felt. She consumed our minds.

It could also have something to do with the fact that I'd

had Billy's mouth around my cock, but more so was that any chance to have Josie in our lives, under our bodies and in our hearts, was worth any risk.

Yeah, it'd be fucked knowing when she was with Billy he'd be in her. However, he already was. He was stuck deep within her mind and heart, like I was.

We needed our light.

We needed our Josie.

I just prayed what I had in mind would work out for the best.

Parking out front instead of under the hotel was going to make it easier to get our shit, make a call and get back to Josie faster. I didn't like leaving Josie on her own, but I knew she didn't live far from her work and I knew we'd make quick work of the crap we had to do. Hell, we'd probably even beat her to work.

Sliding off my girl, I walked into the hotel with a silent Billy behind me. We got in the lift and rode it up to our floor. Panic settled within me. I was fearful he wasn't going to go for it and if he didn't, that would fuck up my chance at our light. I couldn't have that.

As soon as we were in our room, I turned to him, my mouth open ready to plead the advantages of doing it my way. But he got there first, "All right. I'm willin'. Christ, of course I am if it means Josie would be in my life."

I swiped my hand over my mouth to contain the huge fucking smile creeping forward. "Good." I nodded and turned my back on him, heading to the kitchen for something to do.

Billy followed to ask, "You reckon she'll go for it?"

Turning, I placed my arse against the counter and said, "Not sure, but I fuckin' hope so. We need to give her time though. She needs to get used to us being around her all the time."

He nodded and placed his hands in his jean pockets before saying, "We have to show that if either of us touch her, we won't get jealous. She needs to see we're cool with it. Then when she's been used to it for a while, we'll tell her about what we want."

"Deal."

He raised his brows at me and smirked. "You sure you can handle sharing Josie?"

Glaring, I asked, "Can you?"

He snorted. "Yeah, even if I did get jealous, I'd fuckin' hide it 'cause I'd do anything to have Josie. I've always wanted her. I'll be in her, my smell will be on her skin, and I'll be on her mind, even if she's with you. Are you cool with all that?"

"You're the only other brother I'd let this shit happen with. Fuck, we've both been hard for her for a fuckin' long time. This is the best option so we both get to enjoy all that is Josie... *if* she goes for it in the end. So, to answer your question, yeah, I can handle it. You?"

"Hell yeah." He smiled. I shared a grin with him and then pulled my phone from my pocket. "You get our shit packed. I'll call Talon and then we ride back to Josie at her work."

"We ain't sleepin' here?"

Scrunching up my nose, I gave him a what-do-you-think look.

He chuckled and said, "Lookin' forward to bein' around our woman twenty-four seven."

"We take it easy for a while, yeah?"

"Course," he replied before walking out of the kitchen.

With my phone to my ear, I waited for Talon to answer, he did after three rings with, "Talk."

"Situation's fucked up. Some guys at her school think she's their play thing. Always in her space and teasin' her. We roughed one up today when we saw it. Fuck, Talon, she had a look of terror in her eyes… until she saw us. The one today said he'd back off, but apparently, there's a bigger arsehole we gotta deal with."

"Then deal."

"We will, but now we have Josie sayin' she doesn't want us to stay, doesn't want you put out by havin' two of your employees takin' a break. She was gonna ring you herself and ask for a prospect to come here. She realises she needs help now, thank fuck."

"She's too damn nice. Tell her you're both stayin'. I need men at the Caroline Springs charter. Memphis tells me shit's goin' down there, so I've been thinkin' anyway to send brothers his way. After Josie's shit is dealt with, you head to the compound. I'm also sendin' Dodge your way with Dallas, as well as Saxon. He'll be finished with his probation time of being a prospect soon anyway. Lan is also gettin' promoted to a position in that area, so if you need help, he'll have your back."

Lan was Stoke's cousin and a detective. He used to be a stickler for rules, but ever since shit went down with Malinda, he's been a different person. He was still a cop, but since realising we didn't deal in bad shit, he made the choice to have the Hawks members' backs if any crap like that went down again.

"Done. Though, boss, she's thinkin' of movin' back after her schoolin' is done. She's gonna try and finish early."

"We want her back, but don't she like it there?"

"Not sure. I think 'cause of all her shit, she's scared… but hell, we've only been around her today, and Billy and I can see she's grown. She's a minx when she wants to be. Those fuckers are what's holdin' our Josie back."

"Our?"

Shit.

"Fuck, brother—"

"I mean—"

"I know what you mean," Talon growled. "Christ, we all see you and Billy have a thing for her and she has one for the both of you. She'll wake up soon enough. But either of you fuck her up in any way… I'll deal with you."

"What're you sayin', boss?" I got the "he'd deal with us" part, but the rest.

"I'm saying, Josie needs to live her life how she wants it. I was wrong in tellin' you to get her back here. I think she was ready to come home because she thinks *you boys* are her home. She doesn't realise it yet. She thinks her home is her 'rents, Zara and Mattie. But it ain't. It's the two of you and it has been since she set her eyes on you two. If this shit in the

Caroline Springs charter is deep and fucked up as I think it is, then I need the both of you there for a while. Josie will soon see that her home is with the two of you, so I'm guessin' she won't be makin' that move back to Ballarat unless you're both with her."

Consider my fucking fucked-up mind blown.

"I…. Fuck, I don't know what to say to that."

"Don't say anything. Just know you'd both better make my sister-in-law's world a happy one."

"That's what we're aiming for already."

"Good. I'll have Dodge bring more of your shit and Billy's," he barked and then hung up the phone.

Billy walked into the kitchen with both our bags over his shoulders. "What?" he asked.

"Huh?"

"What the fuck is up with that face?"

By that I knew he meant my clenched jaw, my fucking wide eyes, but also the smile that was playing on my lips. "We're stayin'."

"Yeah, I guessed that. What the fuck, Pick?" He threw the bags down and stood across from me with his hands balled into fists.

"Talon wants us to stay and attend to shit at the Caroline Springs charter when Josie's shit is done."

"All right, that's cool, but… "

"He's okay with us and Josie," I blurted and then tried to control the laughter wanting to bubble out like some kid on hooch because the look on Billy's face was laughable.

"You sayin' you told him our deal? You fuckin' crazy?" he yelled. Yeah, obviously he'd been thinking along the lines I had, that Talon would cut us up good and proper for even thinking of sharing Josie.

Shaking my head, I said, "Nope."

"Spit it the fuck out so we can get to Josie."

"Apparently, everyone has seen the hard-on we had for Josie, but they also saw that Josie had feelin's for the both of us. Long story short, he's given us the go-ahead to be with Josie. He thinks she'll find her home in us, like we have with her."

"But she's lookin' at movin' back to Ballarat, and if we're here… "

"Boss thinks she won't go anywhere we aren't."

"Holy motherfuckin' shit."

"My thoughts exactly when you walked in."

"Holy shit."

"I know, brother."

"This crap just got real. Nothin's holding us back from her now."

"Nope, but we're still bringin' her into it slow."

"Shit, yeah. Can't scare her off, not when all this could work out for the three of us bein' happy."

"Damn right. Now let's roll, go eat at our woman's diner."

BILLY

Things were finally looking up. When Pick had come to me with the idea of sharing Josie, at first, I thought he was crazy. But really, it was the best fucking idea he'd ever had. Now all we had to do was worry about Josie going for it as well. Damn, I hoped she did. Though it wouldn't be for a while, she, *our woman*, needed to be handled with care. We all knew she'd had no one since that fuckface. And he wouldn't have been good to her, so of course she was going to be apprehensive when it came to things in the bedroom… or the kitchen, living room, over the Harley.

Fuck. Now I was hard from thinking of all the places I wanted to take her.

Still, that wouldn't be happening for a while yet. We needed to give our woman time to get used to seeing us every day. To get used to us being around her, wanting to touch her in innocent ways before it escalated into more.

I'd do anything for Josie and if that meant sharing her and waiting, then fuck yes, I would do it.

No matter the amount of blue balls I had to suffer through.

Looking to Pick riding in front of me on his Harley, I thought, like him, he was the only brother that I'd be willing to share Josie with. What helped was the stuff we'd been through and the fact that Josie already had feelings for the both of us. Not saying it was going to be easy watching them together or when they were having their own alone time. Still, it'd be easier knowing she was with a man who cared for her as much as I did. We both wanted the best for her and we both thought we could give her that.

Damn, I hoped she went for it.

Pick already knew where Josie worked from Nancy. We pulled our rides up out front in one of the few spare parks. Looked to be a busy day. Without words, we stalked our way to the diner. Upon opening the door, we heard yelled, "Leave her be, young man."

Our gazes settled on what was before us and knowing Pick, because like me, we didn't like what we saw. In fact, anger rumbled up and shot out of my chest on a roar, "Get the fuck away from her."

Josie was being held around the waist by some dick sitting in a booth. An older lady, no doubt her boss, was standing in front, but off to the side, so I could see the panicked look on Josie's face.

"Josie, here now," Caden growled. Josie went to get up, but fuck-head tightened his grip on her waist.

The diner was quiet, and fuck it to hell, nearly full. The damage I wanted to do to the fucker wasn't going to happen when so many witnesses were around.

Caden's hand touched my back before he started for the table. That touch told me to check my anger, told me to be calm and not hot-headed about it, like I fucking wanted to be. Damn it.

With clenched hands, I walked after Caden, dodging through the tables and chairs scattered around. Some of the idiot's mates eyed us and I got a thrill when their eyes landed on our vests.

Yeah, motherfuckers, look who you got to deal with.

One pansy even stood, muttering, "I'm not getting involved in this." Then left as Caden and I stopped just in front of their booth.

"I don't want trouble in here," the old lady said.

"We ain't bringin' it, and it'll stay that way if this… guy let's go of something that belongs to us."

"Cameron, they're from Hawks," a mate of Cameron's who sat across from him in the booth uttered.

Cameron, ignoring all of us, said to Josie, "Sugar, I didn't know you were a club whore." He grabbed her chin and roughly pulled it around so she was looking at him.

It took everything in me not to jump the table and kill the fucker.

Take a blade to his neck.

Gut him like the pig he was.

"And yet you won't put out for me. Stupid slut."

"Enough," I growled low. Caden stepped to the side and I stepped up. My hands went to the table and I leaned in, over Josie, to get in this guy's face where I whispered, "Listen here, you little shit. You do not speak to her like that. She ain't no club whore. She's our boss' sister-in-law. You know what that means? She's like a fuckin' princess to us and anyone who gives her shit has us to deal with. Do you know what that means?"

The fool smirked at me and said, "No, what?"

"Let her up and I'll enlighten you."

"Billy," Caden warned.

Looking over my shoulder, I said, "I'll do it in the nicest possible way, brother." Caden snorted and shook his head. He reached his hand out to Josie. I moved back and thank fuck, the dickhead let her up. She went straight into Caden's arms. She was safe, for now. But something told me, no matter what I was about to say to the cum-sucker, he wouldn't take the threat real.

I was looking forward to delivering some pain then.

"Well?" Cameron mocked.

Shaking my head, I smiled down at him. The cocky smirk fell from his lips for a second. I leaned back in, met his gaze and held it with a glare while I told him the truth. "It means, *Cameron*, that if you continue this shit for our princess, then expect payback. And I mean payback in the form of pain. And *that*, Cameron, means you won't be walkin' for the rest of your life, 'cause I will have shoved that much shit down your throat and up your arse you won't want to sit down or eat. You'll want your life to end and quickly, but I won't bring the quick and painless end to you. No. Once I'm done, I'll give you over to our boss, but it won't be only him. You see, you little fuckin' twat, there're thousands of us who like to dish out pain when retaliating against a dipshit who has harmed a member of our club. You will be beaten, abused and tortured—"

"Billy, that'll do," Caden snapped.

Looking over my shoulder, I saw Josie's shocked gaze as

she clung to Caden. Fuck. I was a stupid fucking idiot, not thinking Josie would have heard anything I just said.

Christ. I probably just scared her half to death. Now she knew I could be one disgusting, mean motherfucker.

"That was… crude, but to the point, kid." Turning to Josie's boss who, fuck me, was smiling wide, she clapped me on the back and then said to Cameron, "Now get outta here, boy, and never grace this establishment again with your bad temper. This is a safe place for my girl, Josie, so I better not see your face in here again or I'll be telling these guys."

Cameron glared up at Josie's boss and said, "You're picking the wrong side, Marybeth."

"No, boy." She shook her head sadly. "You are. You can't keep hidin' behind your daddy all your life."

We all moved back when Cameron started to shift out of the booth. Caden quickly placed Josie behind him and stood with his arms over his chest. I was surprised when they all left quietly, his mates following behind like the sheep they were.

As soon as the front door closed after them, Josie stepped out and started, "Marybeth—"

Only Marybeth put her hand up in Josie's face. "Don't want to hear it. I should have done something a long time ago. I saw what he did to you, the way you'd enter your shell when he was around, but I didn't have the balls to do anything… until now. You keep these boys close, Josie."

"But don't you understand, you standing up to him in front of people… he could—"

"I don't care what he can do. No longer, sweetpea, okay.

This place is safe for you. Now get your arse home. Take the evening off."

With worried eyes, Josie sent Marybeth a small appreciative smile and started for the door. Caden was right behind her and I would have been until a small hand wrapped around my arm to halt me.

Turning, I faced Marybeth, I was shocked for the third time that day when she whispered, "For the first time, that girl out there came into work with a skip in her step and a smile on her beautiful face. Not until I saw the two of you come in here and do what you did for her did I know why her mood suddenly changed. I wish I had the guts a long time ago to rip that boy a new one like you just did, but I didn't. Thank you, kid. Thank you for bringing the Josie I knew she could be to the front. Thank you for being such a badarse and teaching that boy a lesson. However, I'm not sure that boy is smart enough for that lesson to sink in. Tell me, you boys are stickin' close to her?"

"We ain't goin' anywhere 'til her shit's done. Or at all."

She nodded to the floor and then looked back up and met my stare. "Does she know you both love her?"

My head flinched back an inch in shock.

What. The. Fuck.

Marybeth giggled and then sobered. "Kid, it's written all over your face, and his. You give her time and I swear, from what I saw today, she will love you both back just as hard." My nose screwed up. How could an old lady think it was right for Josie to love two guys?

Marybeth scoffed in my face. "Don't look like that. Josie

is full of heart and warmth. That girl has been living on the doorstep of hell. There's something in her eyes that tells me as much. She deserves happiness and, if the two of you can give that to her, then everyone will understand. If no one gets it... fuck 'em. Fuck anyone who thinks different."

That was when I burst out laughing.

CHAPTER SEVEN

JOSIE

I had never heard Eli speak like that before. I knew motorcycle men were different from most average men. I knew when they protected, they did it fiercely. I just didn't know that when they wanted to get a point across, they did it in such a way that was crude, mean and vicious.

Was I disgusted with what Eli said?

Yes.

Was I scared by what Eli said?

Yes.

Could I get over what Eli said?

Yes. 100 percent yes. At the time, it was a shock to my fragile system. However, no matter what way I looked at it, I knew he was doing it all for me.

He hated what I was going through, so much so, he let his emotions run him. Those strong, wild emotions were something frighteningly sweet, and I meant 'sweet' because he was doing it for me.

Should I be scared to see that side of him?

No.

How could I when he was doing it all to protect me.

Looking back through the window, I witnessed Eli throw his head back and laugh out loud to something Marybeth said, that sight was beautiful. So even though the words scared me, Eli himself didn't, because I knew I would be safe around him, and Caden.

"Precious, you okay?" Caden asked as we stood outside waiting for Eli.

My gaze went from Eli inside to Caden, and I smiled. "Yes, I'm fine."

He studied my face, looking from my eyes to my mouth and then his lips twitched. "Good." He took my hand in his. I didn't flinch that time. I welcomed it. It was Caden after all and when Eli came out, I could also take his hand, because he was Eli and they were my home.

"Our girl is strong." Caden grinned.

Nodding, I said, "I'm getting there with your help, Eli's, and Simone's. I finally feel I can be." I giggled. "Though, you both better look out when I'm fully there."

He chuckled. "Looking forward to it."

The diner's door opened and out strolled Eli. He ran a hand through his longer hair on top, his sides were shaved. He seemed troubled. Even though he was only just laughing with Marybeth, he seemed as though the weight of the world was on his shoulders. Speaking of his well-defined shoulders, they were slumped slightly. His eyes met mine, but moved away quickly. It was then I knew what was worrying him.

To put his burden at ease, I gave Caden's hand a small squeeze before I let go and turned my whole body to Eli.

"Josie—"

He didn't get to finish because in the next second, I threw my arms around his neck. He fell back a step. His arms went around my waist to steady us. With surprised eyes, he looked down at me. "Sweetheart?"

"Whatever you're thinking, don't."

"But—"

"No. Yes, your words were... violent and frightening, but I know,"—I touched my chest—"I know deep in here that you would never hurt me. I know, Eli, you talk the talk and you may show it, you may beat a person up. But it wouldn't be someone who didn't deserve it. It wouldn't be someone who hadn't done wrong by you or your brothers. What you did, what you said was hard to hear, but no matter what, I *know* you are a good man. Don't let your mind tell you that I think any differently of you. I don't. You're still my Eli." I smiled.

He closed his eyes; however, before he did, I didn't miss the softness in them. I also didn't miss the gratitude he felt from my words.

It was obvious he didn't think of his next move.

His forehead came forward and touched mine. His hand

came up and slid to the side of my neck. His other arm wound around my waist and he pulled me in close. So close the front of our bodies touched. All the while his eyes stayed closed and mine stayed opened, so I witnessed the panic hit him. His eyes flashed open and he stepped back.

"Shit, Josie, sorry. I... ah... I shouldn't have done that."

Silly man. Didn't he understand and know I didn't mind? It was as though something inside of me had all of a sudden —since these two men rode into town—snapped, and the gentle touches Caden and Eli delivered were like a breath of fresh air against my skin. Maybe it was because I had missed them so.

Maybe it was because my body craved attention and it knew that Caden and Eli would treat me with care.

Or maybe it was because my heart was involved when it came to the both of them.

I wanted their touch.

I wanted their eyes on me.

And I wanted them to care for me as much as I did them.

To show it, I stepped up to Eli, took his hands in mine and slowly, I led one of his hands to my neck again and the other to my waist. To start with, his body was tense. The pulse in his neck beat faster. I wanted to continue watching it, but I could no longer because my body was crushed against Eli's, one arm around the back of my head, the other tightly secured around my waist.

"Sweetheart," he breathed.

I tilted my head and whispered against his ear, "You and Caden. Only the two of you am I comfortable to have touch my skin. They say absence makes the heart grow fonder, maybe that's the case here. Whatever it is, I can't be sure. All I do know is when you and Caden are close, when you brush by me or reach for me, I don't cower. I may flinch sometimes, but I don't ever cower."

"Sweetheart," he repeated. His voice held so many emotions. The main one was awe.

"You guys mean so much to me. You must know this by now?"

He chuckled. "Well, no, babe, we've only been reunited a day."

I couldn't help but giggle. Pulling back, I smiled up at him. "That's true, but already it feels like you've both been here a lot longer and I suppose that has to do with the fact that you've both always been on my mind."

Caden's heat at my back was the first thing I felt before his hands went to my shoulders. I looked over at him and when I did, he said, "Like you've been on ours, precious."

A blush took over my cheeks. "Well, that's good to know." With a smile, I stepped away from them both and started toward their rides. "Let's get out of here and find something to eat."

For the first time in quite some time, I'd finally felt light. It was as though the big bag of sorrow was no longer pressing against my skin, heart and soul.

Finally, I felt like I could smile, laugh and cherish the days that would follow.

We decided, after the guys took me for a ride through the city, to get some takeaway and go home. When we'd stopped at St. Kilda beach, I quickly texted Simone and told her our plan. She suggested to get Chinese delivered. The guys were happy with that, so I left her our order. As we rode back to the apartment, I couldn't help but think about the fact that I wasn't missing home as much. Of course I still missed my parents. They were, after all, the ones to show me—with the help of Zara and Mattie—not all people in the world were doom and gloom. A big need to see them was still inside of me; however, the urgency of it had been taken away when I saw two, glorious bikers walking my way.

Why two?

Why were those two men important to me more than… anything?

Because they mean so much to me.

Because they know what I am.

They know I'm damaged.

Dark and damaged.

And yet, here they were.

They knew everything about me, everything that had happened to me and yet, they were still there for me. Still willing to do anything for me and *still* caring about me.

They were my ending.

They were my life.

My home.

I had been denying myself in many ways… but no more.

WE WERE HAVING a great time sitting around the table,

eating, laughing and talking. Simone, I could see, had fallen in lust with Eli and Caden. Of course, Eli knowing this, suddenly thought it hot in the apartment so he disrobed his cut and then tee. Really, it was comical. When Simone's eye popped wide, her mouth dropped open, and she lost the food that she'd been chewing onto her lap.

Caden burst out laughing. Eli sat back in his chair chuckling and ran his hand down his defined tattooed chest and six pack of abs. "See something you like?" He winked at her.

Of course, I had to go and ruin the moment. Because when I heard those words and saw Simone nod unconsciously, my heart squeezed tight in my chest and I felt the colour drain from my face. My gaze went straight to my plate and I stared numbly down at it as thoughts bombarded my brain.

Eli deserved someone experienced.

I couldn't openly gape at him like Simone and tell him that I liked what I saw because I would fumble around it. I would blush and probably run from the room because I had been caught ogling his magnificent body.

I was pathetic.

I was still a child really.

I knew nothing about love making, passion or anything that involved being with someone.

God, I couldn't even tell them I wanted them *that* way.

I would be useless for them.

They deserved better than the fumbling fool I was.

I was twenty-one for God's sake and I was useless in an intimate situation.

Eli should go for someone like Simone.

And Caden... he should find someone who would be perfect for him.

Not someone who was damaged.

God. Who was I kidding?

Why had I even thought I could... what? Be with them? Have them both and be the greediest bitch there was by taking their own chance of happiness away for my own pitiful sake.

"We should talk about bed arrangements." Simone's voice penetrated my thoughts. "You guys could crash in mine. I wouldn't mind at all."

"You couldn't handle us," Caden teased.

No, but she would give it a try and you would probably be impressed with what she came up with. Not like anything I could show them.

Why did I think I could have this happiness?

Wow, it was only hours ago I was ready to stop denying what I wanted, but when reality crashed in... it gutted me.

Even if they were my home.

They deserved better than what I could ever give them.

"I can't..." ...*do it to them.*

"Josie?" Simone called.

They needed someone experienced. Someone better.

"Sweetheart?"

It would be best if they left.

I was wrong, so very wrong. I couldn't do it to them. I couldn't drag them down into my dark.

Blinking rapidly, I took a deep breath and sat straight. "I-I think I need to go to bed."

Simone giggled. "We were just talking about that."

Trying for a smile, it failed, and she saw it.

"Girl, you know I don't mean anything. I don't want them."

A snort came out of me before I could stop it. Was she crazy? Who wouldn't want them? No one.

"Josie," she demanded.

I nodded instead of saying anything and stood from the table. Then I shrugged. "Not that I'd care anyway." Oh, God, that was harsh. It was bitchy and not me, but it was for the best.

"What the fuck, Josie?" Eli hissed.

"Billy," Caden growled low.

"No, I want to know what she meant by that," Eli barked and banged a fist on the table.

"I need some sleep," I stated with no emotion, again not me. I was breaking on the inside, but I thought if I changed, if I showed them I didn't care, they would leave, they would find their happiness.

Starting for the doorway, I made it two steps before a hand grabbed my upper arm. Looking to it and then following it up, I saw it was Caden and he was smiling.

I shook my head, confused. Why was he smiling?

"Hang on there, precious," he said before turning to Simone. "Can you leave for a while?" And then he turned to

Eli. "You, sit the fuck down and control your fuckin' temper."

"Girl, you better be back to yourself in the morning or we're having words, and you won't like them. This isn't you, Josie, and I don't like seeing it." Simone glared and then walked from the room.

"Pick?" Eli said.

Only Caden ignored him. Instead, he tugged on my arm enough to throw me off balance and I collided with his body. His hand went under my chin and forced my gaze up to meet his amused one.

"Baby," he started. "You forgetting I been where you have? I know the way your brain works and when that shit started with the flirtin', your brain went to another world. A world where you think Eli and I could use someone like your housemate. Someone who isn't... and fuck, I hate to say it, but damaged like you have been. What you don't get, precious, is that we both are damaged in one way or another, like you. We now know we have to be careful when we're around you. We were just tryin' to make your house-mate think we're okay guys for *you*." My eyes widened. "Yeah, baby, you. It's only ever been you for us. Precious, like you said to Eli, we've always been on your mind and I told you you've been on ours, but what I didn't say was... you consumed it."

My heart beat like crazy behind my ribs. The rise and fall of my chest was erratic because of my breathing.

"Now, I guess it's the best time to tell you. Josie, we ain't goin' anywhere—"

"Pick," Eli growled in warning.

Warning for what?

Caden turned his handsome face from mine to Eli. "S'okay, man. She needs to know where we stand. She needs this, so her mind can't play tricks on her again about us."

Goodness. Where was this going?

"Precious, Billy and I are staying here in Melbourne. We're stayin' here until your shit is over—"

"But—"

"No, baby, we're stayin' and then when your shit's over, we're gonna keep stayin' here to help Memphis out with some stuff, which could take a while." He stopped to study me.

They were staying here, in Melbourne with me, but why? Was it an order from Talon?

"Even if Talon didn't want us to stay here, we would've." Was he a mind reader? "Baby." He waited until I was looking up at him again. "We'd stay for you, Josie."

"I-you, both of you... I can't." What was I trying to say?

"Sweetheart," Eli uttered as he walked up to our sides. He took my hand in his as I looked to him. "You're it for us."

"No," I whispered. "You both deserve so much more."

"Honey, that's bullshit," Eli said gently. My brows rose and he ran a finger over them. "You've known how we've felt for a fuckin' long time. We've stated that from the start. What you need to know now, is that, for you, for all of us so we can have our happiness in life, we're willing to both be with you."

I gasped. Was this for real? "But... isn't that wrong?"

"No, woman. What we feel for you is not wrong. We'll take this slow, very slow. We'll work it all out together."

They were both willing to go slow for me. They both wanted me and no one else. They were both willing to put up with each other so they both could have me... just like I wanted them both.

"Precious, do you want that? Do you want us?"

"W-what about what people will think?"

"We don't give a fuck what other people think. If this works with the three of us, then you shouldn't give a fuck either. Baby, we're willing to put our all in if you are. You're it for us, Josie," Caden said.

"I-um, this. I... you both."

"Spit it out, honey, so we can all crash. Been a big day," Eli teased.

Smiling shyly, I told them, "I would like to see... slowly, if this could work."

"Fuck yeah." Caden grinned and gave me a squeeze.

"Four years of waiting, sweetheart, and finally you can be ours." Eli smiled widely.

Too many emotions were clouding me. I couldn't stop grinning. But worry also taunted me with what could go wrong. However, the thrill, one that sent a shiver through my body, of knowing they wanted me as much as I did them was winning.

It could work. It had to work. I'd loved them for so long and kept them both at arm's length because I was didn't want to hurt one of them... but now. Goodness, now they wanted to work it out between the three of us.

My life was coming together, and it started when the two men, who owned my heart for so long, walked back into my dark life.

I was silent as they ordered me off to bed, both smirking at my smiling face. Caden was the first to kiss my cheek and then Eli.

"What about you both?" I asked.

"We'll alternate. I'll take the couch tonight and Eli can have Parker's bed until we find a place of our own."

My head went back on my shoulders, "You mean...?"

Caden chuckled. "Baby, get your cute arse to bed. That's something we can talk about another day."

With a quick kiss to each of their cheeks, I strode from the room. My mind was already consumed, so the thought of moving in together was definitely going to have to take a shelf for a later date... a date when we knew what was happening between us would work.

CHAPTER EIGHT

JOSIE

Friday I woke to Simone jumping on my bed. Once I was coherent enough, she demanded to know what was up with my attitude the previous night. I explained everything, all the thoughts I had flowing through my head. How I thought I didn't deserve the attention of the two men.

She cackled and said, "Honey, you're crazy. I knew they were all talk. Christ, any female can see how they feel about you. It's hard for them to even take their eyes off you." She beamed and squealed.

Which was when my bedroom door burst open and in it stood Caden and Eli wearing nothing but boxers. Their chests rose and fell rapidly and their guns were drawn to the room.

Simone burst out laughing, laying across my bed holding her stomach.

I offered a grimace and a shrug. "Sorry, um, she was excited about something at school today."

Caden relaxed first and with a smirk, as though he knew I was lying and had been in fact talking to her about them, shook his head and left the room.

Eli rolled his eyes and placed his hands to his waist, still holding his gun. Before he wandered off, he muttered, "All women are crazy."

The morning started out frantic, after Simone and I took the time to talk, we realised we were late for class. We quickly dressed, me in jeans, a tee and a jacket, while Simone went for a skirt, tights and a woollen jumper. The guys stood waiting, with smirks on their handsome faces, while we rushed around the house getting organised. On the way out, I grabbed a banana for breakfast and climbed into the passenger side of Simone's car. When the back door opened, I jumped and looked behind me to see Eli climbing in the car.

"W-what are you doing?" I asked.

"Babe." He smiled. "You didn't honestly think we'd let you go to uni on your own? I'm doing half the time and Caden will catch up later."

"But, why?"

"Sweetheart, no one fucks with you. We need to make sure all those fuckers got the picture or else they deal with us." He reached out and gently touched my shoulder before pulling his hand back and saying, "Don't stress, Josie. I won't even be in your classes. I'll wait outside for them to finish."

"This is going to be so much fun." Simone clapped, started the car and began to drive.

"But... " I started before shoving the banana in my mouth and doing up my seat belt.

"Seriously, babe. Just go with it."

It wasn't like I had a choice, really.

Remaining silent, I smiled. If I were honest with myself, I was glad there wasn't a choice. I had been worried with how the day would turn out. Knowing Cameron, he would be fuming over the altercation they had the previous day.

Having Eli at my back eased my troubled thoughts.

It wasn't until lunch did I find out how difficult it was to have Eli with me. He stayed true to his words and stayed outside the lecture room. However, the looks he got from the female students irritated me. I knew there were many good-looking women around and they'd zoned in on the rough, handsome biker.

Never had I had so many girls come up to me in class to see if I could introduce them to Eli. When I didn't respond, they glared at me. I felt bad for the barest of heart beats, but that quickly passed as I didn't want Eli to think I was pushing other women onto him, not when my feelings for him were strong.

Groaning, I got up from my seat and walked out of the room. It was my last class before lunch and then after, I had only one other, but that would go for another two hours.

As soon as I passed the door, I spotted Eli standing

opposite me, only he was surrounded by at least five women. I grumbled under my breath. I wanted to stomp my foot, waltz over there and stake my claim.

But I didn't.

"Hey," someone said beside me.

Looking up, I quickly took a step back. A guy I didn't know stood before me. "Um, hi."

He smiled. "Sorry to scare you. I'm Kevin." Thankfully he didn't hold out his hand to me. "I'm in a few classes of yours and, ah, sorry I wanted to see, uh, now that you're not, um with Cameron."

I gasped. "I was never with him."

"Sorry." He blushed. "I know, what I mean is, I heard Cameron has backed off and, now that he has, I wanted to know if you would like to... go out to the movies or something."

"No," a voice growled. We both looked to Eli standing beside us.

"Who are you?" Kevin asked.

"I'm hers and she's mine. Not only that, she belongs to Hawks."

My head went back. *I'm his and he's mine?*

"Billy, are you coming to have lunch with us?" a girl called.

"No," Eli snapped, his gaze never leaving Kevin.

I watched as the girl and her friends pouted and then glared at me, walking off.

"Okay, I'm gonna head off," Kevin said.

"Good," Eli stated in a short snap, crossing his thick arms over his chest.

Before Kevin got to step away, Caden appeared at his back. "Problem here?" Caden growled.

Goodness.

"No," I squeaked. "Kevin was just leaving." With a nod, Kevin quickly shuffled away from Caden, turned and stalked out of the school.

"What was that about?" I demanded to Eli.

"Babe," was all he said.

Frustrating man.

I started down the hall, making my way to the cafeteria for lunch when Caden asked, "What did that guy want?"

"He asked Josie out on a date."

"What the fuck?" Caden growled.

Spinning to face them, I glared. "Well, it's not like Eli hasn't had a busy morning and now you're here, the women will go extra crazy. I've lost count of the times they've asked me for Eli's number or if he's free to date or why he's here or how they tell me how hot he is. Now they'll do it all over again for you as well, Caden." I growled under my breath and turned around, walking off. Frustration over everything was winning, causing me to react like a little jealous school girl.

Their laughter followed me as I entered the cafeteria and then there was silence. All eyes were on us. For once I didn't cower and slink away. I stood tall and got in the line. Eli and Caden were right behind me.

I was looking down at the selection when someone in

front of me cleared their throat. Looking up, I blanched when another male I didn't know smiled down at me.

"Hey, I'm Tony. I was wondering if you're free this weekend?"

Goodness me.

Did everyone know that Cameron had backed off? And now the men were confident in approaching me?

That was until Eli and Caden's heat touched my back. Their arms were folded over their chests as they stared down Tony.

"Are they your bodyguards or something?" Tony asked.

"No," Caden growled.

"Brothers?" Tony asked.

"Fuck no," Eli snapped.

"Just back the fuck off and tell any fool who tries to ask Josie out, they'll have us to deal with," Caden ordered.

Heck. Shaking my head, I grabbed my tray and went to the nearest vacant table. I slammed my tray down and sat.

Too late I realised I only grabbed an apple. Shrugging to myself, I picked it up and took a bite. Juice dribbled down my chin. I wiped it away as Eli sat on one side of me and Caden the other side.

"You'll need more than that," Caden said and placed two pizza slices on my tray.

"Thank you," I uttered.

"Precious, we're only looking out for you."

"I know, but—"

"Hey, girlfriend." A leggy blonde smiled at me as she stopped in front of our table. Inwardly, I groaned. I had never met this woman before and yet she was calling me girlfriend. "I'm having a party this weekend. I wanted to know if you all want to come?"

"What's in it for us?" Eli smiled. Quickly, the smile faded, he turned an apologetic grimace to me as I glared back. I suppose I couldn't expect to turn his playboy attitude off overnight. At least he felt bad for it.

Glancing back at the blonde, I said, "No, but thank you for asking." I smiled.

"That's cool, how about just your friends come then?"

I really wanted to bang my head against the table. Instead, I took my annoyance out on the pizza and bit into it roughly.

"We're busy," Eli said.

"Yeah, anything I could help out with?" she purred.

Snorting, I took another bite of my pizza.

"Do you have a problem?" she asked me.

Sighing, I placed my pizza down on the plate and looked back up to her. "No, I don't, but I think you're trying too hard. Yes, they're hot men, but they have already said they were busy and you're still trying to throw yourself at them." Slamming my mouth shut, I blushed. Never had I spoken that much to someone I didn't know, especially so confrontationally.

I was appalled by my behaviour.

Then again, I didn't like the way she wanted a chunk out of Eli and Caden.

"Scat," Eli growled.

She huffed and stormed back to her table.

"Sweetheart—"

"I can't believe I just said that," I uttered.

"Baby," Caden started. "You think we're hot?"

Blushing, I was glad, for once, when we were interrupted again.

"Hey all, you would not believe the rumours I've been hearing starring our little girl here," Simone said as she sat across from us. She looked to my blushing cheeks and asked, "What's going on?"

Eli chuckled, leaned back in his seat and said, "Not much. Women keep hittin' on us. Josie doesn't like it. She told one girl to stop. Plus Josie thinks we're hot."

"Eli," I snapped.

"Precious," Caden said in a low tone. Turning my head, he moved in closer, so our noses nearly touched. "We like that you don't like women tryin' to sink their claws into us. Shows us that you do want us. So maybe, if it happens, you tell the leeches we're your fellas."

"Um." I blushed, my breathing heavy. "O-okay."

"Good." He smiled and tucked a loose piece of hair behind my ear sending tingles down my body. He caught that shudder and his smile deepened.

Shaking myself out of the daze, I glanced at Simone and asked, "So, what're the rumours?" before I picked up my pizza and started eating it again.

"Damn, woman. You're so freaking lucky," she said, glancing from Caden to Eli. "Just from the looks they give you I could come in my pants."

"Simone," I snapped.

She shook her head. "What? Woman, don't fret about the other hussies. The way these guys are with you, they'll get the picture."

"Simone. Rumours?"

"Oh, yeah. The others aren't worth mentioning, but I'll tell you my favourite. Your boys here are a part of the mob. They think you're a daughter of some drug lord and they're here to protect you. Also, seems Cameron isn't here today. They're saying they killed him." She shrugged and started on her pasta salad.

Goodness.

Rumours I could handle. The torment before was something I couldn't. Let them believe what they wanted. I no longer cared.

CHAPTER NINE

JOSIE

*T*he next month flew by. And most of it was shared with happy thoughts and memories.

The first weekend was spent lounging around. The times we did venture out was to take a ride on their Harleys. Sunday morning, early hours, I woke to find myself on the couch asleep with my two men beside me. My head was resting on Eli's shoulder, his arm slung loosely around my waist as he slouched down on the couch. My legs and one hand were behind me laying upon Caden. His body was also slouched, but both hands were warming my legs. I was worried they were uncomfortable, but I liked the position I was in, surrounded by the two most special men in my life. So it wasn't hard for me to curl back into Eli and fall back asleep.

University was amazingly peaceful over the month. Cameron was smart enough to stay away from me, though it didn't stop the deathly glares I received from him every time we had class together or he spotted us walking around campus. He'd also advised his friends to stay away from me. I was having more fun each day I went to uni and I wished I had said something to someone back home a long time ago, even before Simone had taken the matter into her own hands.

I'd been suffering for nothing.

Something I would regret for a while yet.

For the first two weeks, things between the guys and myself were relatively sweet. They would hug me, touch me gently with a light caress or kiss my cheek, forehead and neck.

Then Caden, ten days ago, came to me and told me we were going out on a date. Of course my heart began to beat fast in excitement, but nerves fluttered in my stomach too. Where would they expect the date to end? In bed together? I wasn't sure I was ready for that.

After I dressed in jeans and a nice fitted shirt with a jacket over the top, I walked from my bedroom to find Caden already standing by the door and Eli sitting on the couch.

"Ready?" Caden asked.

Smiling, I nodded and walked to his outstretched hand to grab hold of it. My other hand slid around his forearm.

"We'll be back later."

I turned, expecting Simone to be there, even though I

knew she'd already gone out. So when I didn't see her, confusion swept through me. Who had Caden been talking to?

"No worries," Eli responded.

My eyes widened. "You're not coming?"

He gave me a wink. "No, sweetheart, this is Caden's and your night. I've got tomorrow night with you."

Goodness. Now I was a ball full of more nerves than before.

Caden and I would be alone for the first time since they'd arrived.

Alone.

Would he try to kiss me?

Oh, I hoped so... even though the thought sent butterflies to assault my stomach.

Still, I hadn't gone without Eli before and I was worried he would be hurt over my time with Caden. Would he be jealous and end up lashing out in some way?

"Babe," Eli called. I then watched him stand from the couch and stalk toward me. He cupped my cheeks and smiled reassuringly down at me. "I love that you're worried about going out without me, but you and Pick need this, like I'll need it tomorrow night. We need our time as a couple instead of the three of us."

"But—"

"Sweetheart," he interrupted. "I'm not sayin' I don't like the times when it's the three of us. But I think, to make this work, we need... fuck, I'm gonna sound like a chick. We need our separate date nights."

Caden coughed a laugh into his hand. "Yep, chick soundin' right there, brother."

Eli rolled his eyes. "Fuck off, you agreed with me."

Out of the corner of my eye, I caught Caden's gaze. "You did?"

"Of course, baby. Billy may be an idiot most of the time, but sometimes he can get somethin' right."

Eli's hand slid from my face to my shoulders. "Sweetheart, I need you to do somethin' for me."

He sounded so serious that I asked straight away, "What?"

"Hit him." With his head, he gestured to Caden. I giggled when I saw his mouth twitch, showing me he was joking.

"Precious won't do that."

Eli leaned forward, his lips swiftly touched my neck, and then he whispered, "Have a good night, babe, and no worryin' about me. Just enjoy it, okay?"

He pulled back to look down at me. "Okay, Eli," I whispered.

That night Caden took me out on our first official date and it was totally different to what Eli and I did together. Caden first took me to a restaurant where we ate seafood, talked and laughed a lot.

He was surprised when I asked him if he thought what we were doing was going to work. His nod was fast and then he said, "Yeah, Josie. I know what I feel for you and I know Billy feels the same way. It helps he's an okay guy and I trust him with you. It'll be good. Christ, fuck that, what we'll have will be fantastic."

My shy smile told him I believed him. If he and Eli could work together to be with me, then I had to stop worrying about the both of them turning against each other for some reason or another. I had to trust them with that, like I trusted them with me.

After eating, Caden took me, in Eli's new truck he bought in the first week of being here, for a drive. At first, I thought he was taking me parking... because wasn't that something couples did?

My men were rough, tough, bikers. No doubt they were feeling frustration in their pants with how slow things were going. And I felt bad for it. Especially when I was the one holding back from them and *then*, I'd witness, some mornings, their morning wood, which they would try to hide while they went to the bathroom. It wasn't only their morning wood I'd been thinking about, but the times when I would sit on the couch with them, or the times I cleaned the apartment and I'd find them watching me while they—what they thought discreetly—adjusted themselves in their jeans.

Though, thinking of their... erections wasn't a good plan on my first date with Caden. When he pulled into the only drive-in theatre, I was thrilled and now turned-on from thinking of them being hard for me.

"Baby, come here," Caden ordered. With sweating palms, a fast beating heart and nerves dancing in my stomach, I slid along the seat to the middle one, right next to him.

Only I panicked for nothing, because all he did was draw me into his body by his arm around my shoulders. Then he leaned back and we watched the movie while he shovelled and I nibbled on the popcorn.

My lip was something I also nibbled because I wanted something to happen. I wanted Caden's lips on mine. I wanted to know what they felt like, what they tasted like. I was weary of the forehead and neck kisses. If we were supposed to be a couple, then shouldn't it have advanced already?

Then a thought crossed my mind.

Were they waiting for me to make the move?

Goodness, maybe they were. They said they'd take it slow, but it was becoming too slow.

A frustrated and annoyed groan fell from my lips and filled the truck's cabin.

Why would they do that to me? I was useless in that department. They had to make the move, not me for goodness' sake.

"What's up, precious?" Caden asked, his arm tightening around my shoulders.

Without thinking, I moved forward and twisted around to glare at Caden. His arm fell from my shoulders as he stared back with an amused look upon his face.

"Don't smirk at me, Caden. What were you both thinking? You both know I'm not confident. I need either of you to make the first move. If you leave it up to me, we'll never get there and by God, I want to get there sooner rather than later, no matter how much it scares me, thinking that somehow I will stuff it all up and you and Eli will laugh at my fumbling schoolgirl ways and leave. I—"

I didn't get to finish. Caden's hand went to my neck and I was roughly pulled toward him. There with his lips lightly resting against my mouth, he growled, "Baby, all you had to do was give us a sign, and now you have." He smiled before his mouth crashed down on mine.

David, my captor so many years ago, had never kissed me and I was grateful he hadn't. Because what Caden was doing to me was something special and I was happy to have shared it with him and then, I was excited to share something just as special with Eli the following night.

The kiss wasn't gentle, it was hard and blissful. Caden slanted his head. I followed suit and the kiss deepened when he slid his tongue into my mouth. *Goodness.* He groaned and my hands frantically gripped his tee, never wanting him to move from my mouth again.

Time disappeared as we kissed. When we came up for breath, which I found hard at that moment, the windows were fogged up and people were backing out of the parking area.

"Fuck, precious, you kiss like that I can't wait to see what else you can do."

A blush heated my already warm cheeks. A strong tingle fluttered between my legs, causing me to rub my thighs together. Caden of course saw it and groaned loudly, as though he were in pain.

"Damn, baby, you do that and slow will be something of the past."

Licking my bottom lip, I asked, "So, I, um. Was... did I do okay... kissing?"

His head rocked back on his shoulders, his eyes wide. "Josie, was that your first kiss?"

Looking to my hands on my lap, I nodded.

"Christ," Caden hissed. My gaze went straight up to him. He leaned forward and gently kissed my lips. "My girl, sweet, shy and never been kissed. So glad I got to kiss you first, baby. We won't tell Billy that. But I can honest to God say that, fuck, beautiful, you'll rock Eli's world with that mouth of yours."

My smile was wide and full of happiness. What made it so big was because Caden obviously cared for Eli. He didn't want to tell Eli that he'd taken my first kiss and that was… sweet.

"Can we do it again?" I asked.

Caden ran a hand over his face. "Precious," he groaned. "I'd love to keep neckin' with you, but I only have so much control. How about we drive home and there, fuck, I'll give you a goodnight kiss."

"Okay," I said happily, moving to my seat and pulling on my seat belt. It was then Caden's laughter filled the cabin.

Caden was true to his word. He even walked me to my bedroom door and kissed me speechless and stupid before he gently pushed me into my room and shut the door… only with him on the other side.

Eli's date was a lot of fun. He was wilder than Caden. Where Caden preferred the quiet, Eli preferred the noise, which explained how we ended up at Luna Park in St Kilda. It was early, so we walked around holding hands while checking things out. Eli had me giggling a lot at his antics. He didn't care if he made a fool of himself if it caused me to laugh. He always seemed on a high and I loved that about him.

What I had to watch out for was his short fuse. His temper was never at me. I knew that with my whole being, I was safe with Eli. But if someone jostled me or looked at me wrongly, Eli would snap into the man I saw in Marybeth's diner. Even one time I had to hold him back when a teenager, a kid of about seventeen, walked by with some mates and said something crude, that he wouldn't mind having me in his bed.

Eli spun around and grabbed the kid's tee. "What the fuck did you say?" he hissed in his face.

"Dude, calm down. He was only joking," one of the kid's mates said.

"I don't give a fuck if he was jokin'. Learn some fuckin' manners. She's my woman and I don't like other guys talkin' crap about her."

"Yeah, yeah, all right, brother."

"I ain't your fuckin' brother." Eli jostled the kid back and forth by his tee.

It was then I snapped out of my shock and went to Eli's side. "Stop it," I demanded. "Eli, he *was* only joking around. He meant nothing by it."

"He was—"

"Eli, please just let him go so we can get back to the fun we were having. Please." I reached out and grabbed his arm. He looked at me and let go of the kid straight away. I started for the opposite direction knowing Eli would follow and he did, leaving the group of teens alone.

"Jose—"

Stopping, I turned to face him. "Eli, you can't keep doing that," I said calmly. "Not everyone is out to harm me in some way. They were just teens, Eli, mucking around and having fun. I didn't take offence to it and neither should you."

He took the last step toward me and his hands went to each side of my neck. "Babe, I'm sorry, okay. I know I suck at controllin' myself, but it's because I watched my father verbally abuse my mum for years. He'd never get physical with her, but what he said was enough to get to her. Every fuckin' time it cut her deep and I don't want you to feel that cut. But for you, I will try to curb it… somewhat."

Eli had never spoken of his parents and I was glad he was opening up about them to me. In a way, I could understand his behaviour, but he needed to learn that I was not fragile any longer, not when I had my two knights beside me.

Stepping in close, I wrapped my arms around his firm waist, my head resting against his chest, where I could hear his heart thumping.

Goodness, was my bad-boy biker nervous?

That thought was crazy. He couldn't be.

"Okay, Eli. Thank you for telling me that. Does… is your mum still with your dad?"

"Yeah, sweetheart. I'd asked her to leave many times, but she never will. No matter how much she knew that shit was hard for her kid to hear and see. Which was why I got outta the house so young."

Resting my chin on his chest, I looked up at him. "Sorry you had to deal with that growing up."

"Babe, it was nothin' really. Not fuckin' worth mentionin'. Not when many go through tougher times."

He meant me.

Still, it didn't matter that mine was harder or different. What mattered was that Eli seeing his parents like that hurt him, and I hated that for him.

Sliding my hands up his chest, I watched with fascination as he stopped breathing. His eyes sprung wider and the pulse in his neck jumped.

As soon as my hands were curled into his hair, I pulled him down a little so our lips could touch for the first time. When they did, I withdrew my head a fraction to see his reaction. He let out a huff of air, his arms tightened around my waist and his stare turned heated and hungry right before he leaned in and pressed his lips to mine again.

His tongue slipped out, testing, trying to see if I was ready. When I opened my mouth to run my own tongue with his, he moaned, and the kiss melted into passion.

Eli pulled away first. His hand went to the back of my head where he brought it against his chest. We took our time to catch our breath. "Jesus, sweetheart. Christ. We have to stop before I take you here and now in front of everyone."

Nothing against the idea came to mind at that present time.

"Bloody hell, you saying nothin' says it all. Let's cool our jets and enjoy the night."

"Does that mean you won't kiss me anymore?"

"Fuck no." He laughed.

And he was right. The rest of the night was completed with food, rides, prizes and fun. The best part was when Eli would steal kisses when he could. His lips always seemed to find their way back to me and I was happy to oblige.

I was surprised to find that Caden and Eli kissed so differently. Both could be hard, gentle and delicious. But both in their own amazing way.

Addiction.

They were mine and I was looking forward to the next stage after kissing… hopefully soon.

The rest of the month was spent on uni and work. The guys went separately, because neither one was willing to leave me unguarded, to see Memphis and got themselves situated in Memphis' charter. Apparently, Dodge and Dallas were in town as well now. I was yet to see them myself, but Eli said they'd settled in well at the Caroline Springs compound, though it made me wonder what was actually going down since Talon had sent so many members down our way. One day I would make it over there to see Memphis, Dodge and Dallas, but studying was taking up the rest of the time I had when I wasn't with Eli and Caden.

With everything being so busy, things between the guys and myself hadn't advanced from the hot kisses that drove not only my mind insane, but my body. Each night they would walk me to my room and both of them would kiss me soundly goodnight… then that was it.

Again, were they waiting for me?

I wasn't sure if they were waiting for me to make the first move, or if they were really so tired from everything they'd been doing. Between guarding me and the compound, they seemed strung out.

I didn't find out the other reason they were strung out until two nights later.

Two nights later, my eyes opened wide.

Two nights later, I was taught there was more to what my mind provided.

Two nights later, I walked in on something that made my panties wet in seconds.

CHAPTER TEN

BILLY

*J*osie had gone to the apartment downstairs to help Mrs Evans, the new tenant, with her two-year-old son while Mrs Evans ran to the grocery store. Simone was out with some dude she was seeing at the time. Pick and I were sitting on the couch watching *CSI*. The women of the house hated the show, so we were happy to get the place to ourselves, knowing that Josie was only downstairs safe.

"Saw Cameron the other day," Pick said after taking a pull of his beer.

"Yeah?"

"Yeah, the idiot and two of his friends cornered me in the dunny. Apparently, they thought I was the lesser freak of the two of us."

I busted out laughing, knowing that wasn't true. We were both the same really. When we protected, we did it in the way no fool would want to try shit. The most ruthless way possible.

"What a fuckin' tool," I said. "What'd you do?"

"After I knocked out his friends, I threatened to gut him like the pig he is. To get my point across, he now has a small scrape across his stomach."

Snorting, I asked, "You think he knows we don't fuck around now?"

"Not likely."

"What's up with that fucker? How dumb can one person be?"

"He likes to hide behind his lawyer daddy. He thinks he's invincible."

"Idiot. No one's invincible to Hawks."

"Exactly."

My hands played with my now empty beer bottle. I'd been wanting to ask Pick something for a long time, but fuck, I was a dude and dudes didn't talk about anything but cars, bikes and work.

"What you wanna ask?" Pick questioned. I looked over at him, one brow raised. I swear the dick could read minds sometimes. He lay on the couch, his knees bent and feet up right next to me. Then he spread his legs and smirked up at me.

"You're a fuckin' freak when you do that."

He shrugged. "I know. It's just easy to read you and our girl, that's all. So, you gonna talk or what?"

"Christ, Pick. I don't know... Fuck. Okay, look... do you think? Hell, I've had a hard-on for the last three weeks over our woman. Do you think she's ready to, you know?"

I was waiting for the laugh, the teasing. When it didn't come, I looked over at him. His face was serious. He shrugged and said, "Not sure. She loves the attention we give her already and, fuck, I know she gets excited from it, but I ain't sure she's ready for the next step. Even if *we* are more than ready."

Banging my head against the back of the couch, I said, "My dick has had enough of my hand every fuckin' morning in the shower."

"I know the feeling," Pick uttered.

We went back to watching TV. I was glad to know I wasn't the only one having a hard time. Josie was fucking amazing. She shared her sweetness between the two of us perfectly. Leaving neither of us worrying she cared for the other more. Nope, our woman showed us both the same love.

CSI finished and goddamn *Mork and Mindy* started playing'. There was no way in hell I was sitting through that crap.

"Pass the remote. We ain't watchin' this," I demanded, holding out my hand for the remote sitting behind Pick's head on the armrest of the couch.

"Fuck off, this show's a classic."

"Brother, don't fuck with me. I ain't watchin' it."

Pick chuckled. "Looks like you don't have a choice."

Dammit, he was going to hog the fucking remote and make me suffer through it. Well, screw that. I moved quickly, I was over him reaching for the remote, but the dick was faster. He grabbed it and stretched his arm out further from my reach.

"Give me the fuckin' remote," I snapped.

"Get the fuck off and I'll think about it." Seeing his mouth twitch when I looked down at him, I knew the fucker was full of shit.

Stretching out, my fingers just touched it… but then all thoughts fled my head when I heard Pick let out a strangled, "Jesus."

My cock knew before my brain registered what my body was actually doing and I guessed Pick had just figured it out as well. Motherfucking Christ, in the action of getting the remote, I was suddenly grinding my hips down on Pick's and without knowing it during the struggle, Pick's legs had moved apart to let my weight fall on top of him.

Now I knew I was rubbing my hard-as-fuck cock against his just-as-hard dick I couldn't stop. The friction felt fucking unreal, especially when it wasn't my hand rubbing one off; instead, I was using Pick's body.

"Hell," I growled. My hand fell away from even trying to get the remote, to the armrest above Pick's head as I kept rubbing our cocks together. I looked down at his half-mast eyes. Christ, he was gone as much as I was. I had to stop it though.

But fuck it felt so good.

"Goddamn." I groaned when Pick's hands slapped to my waist and brought my hips down harder as we slid up and down on each other. "We... we need to stop," I hissed through clenched teeth.

Fuck. My balls were shrinking up. I was close to coming. Damn, it had been too long from having a warm body under me, even if I wasn't inside that body, just the friction was enough.

"In a second." Pick glared up at me. He wanted to finish. Hell, I did also, but we shouldn't be doing what we were doing.

No matter how much my cock loved me for it right then.

Something made me look over my shoulder... mother-fucking Christ. Josie stood there, her eyes hooded, her breath rapid and her hands clenched. Blow me the fuck over, it was like she was fighting with herself not to come over.

What would have been the gentleman thing to do was jump off Pick and attend to Josie, but I was too fucking far gone, all I could think about was the release clawing its way out soon.

Leaning down to Pick more, I whispered, "Our girl's watchin'."

"Fuck—"

"She's likin' what she's seein'."

"Ah, Jesus." Pick groaned. Yeah he was feeling what I was. How fucking hot it was having the girl of our dreams watching us and getting off on it.

So much so, I felt my release on the edge. "I'm gonna come." I moaned and I wasn't quiet about it.

"Fuck yeah. Christ, here comes mine." Pick's grip was going to leave bruises tomorrow on my hips, but four more slides up and down, our cocks rubbing in the right spot sent us over the edge and we convulsed and yelled together as we let our loads squirt free into our boxers and jeans.

The need to collapse on top of Pick was heavy. Still, we had our horny girl to deal with. Hell, if I had known our girl would get turned on by watching me rub one off on Pick, then I would have done it a long time ago.

Slowly, I moved back to sit down at the end of the couch and turned my gaze to Josie, who was frozen on the spot just inside the front door. Her fisted hand was over her heart now. Was she trying to slow it?

The only thing that was annoying the hell out of me was the wetness in my jeans. I'd come so hard I swore I'd have a wet patch staining my jeans.

"Sweetheart... " I waited for her eyes to turn to my face and not our groins. "Did you like what you saw?"

"Billy," Pick's voice warned.

"I-um." Josie licked her lips. Yeah, she liked it a hell of a lot. "Y-yes."

With that word, Pick sat up quickly with a smug smile on his face. "Precious, how did you like it?"

"W-what do you mean?" Her head turned on its side while she thought about Pick's question.

"Babe," I started, her eyes went to me. "Are you wet?"

"Oh," she gasped. Our girl, so sweet, so shy and nervous. "Um… yes. Shouldn't I be?" she asked with worry lacing her voice.

Pick stood first and walked to her. His hands cupped her face before he brought her face up and he touched his lips with hers. "Some women would get off on seein' that. We weren't sure if you would. But we're glad you did."

"You are?" she asked on a whisper.

"Yeah, sweetheart," I said, stepping up to them. Pick moved back so Josie could see me. "Now the question is," I began, but then leaned in to kiss her. Christ, when her tongue peeked out to touch my bottom lip, I deepened the kiss. She was more than ready for the next small stage. One hand grabbed her arse and I pulled her closer, a mew spilled from her mouth that was still attacking mine.

With regret, I moved my mouth from her lips to nibble down her neck. I gestured to Pick to move closer. He did. He stepped up to Josie's other side and as her neck was arched for my kisses, Pick took her lips and she moaned. She was in the moment, feeling instead of thinking. If we could keep her there, she would love it.

Pulling my head back so I could watch Pick and Josie kiss, because it turned me the fuck on, again my dick grew with eagerness. Especially when I saw Pick's hand move up her waist to run over Josie's breast.

"Yes," she mumbled against his lips and that, of course, gave him the sign to keep going. His hand quickly slid down and then up under her tee where he took her breast in hand.

His lips moved from her mouth. He rested his forehead against hers as their heavy breaths got under control.

"Maybe we should move this to the bedroom," I suggested. Josie's nod was subtle, but it was there. Pick removed his hand and grabbed hers to lead her to her bedroom where I was already making my way down the hall. "I'm just gonna change my pants," I said, moving into Parker's room where Pick's and my clothes were held.

"I'll do mine when you get back," Pick said, his voice deeper than usual, lust riding it.

After a quick change and clean up, I made my way into Josie's room only wearing black boxers. I wasn't sure Jose was ready to see me totally naked.

Motherfucking God. When I walked in, it was to see them laying out on the bed. Pick had his upper body over Josie's and his mouth was attacking hers again while his hand inched up her tee. Seeing them like that was the hottest thing I'd ever seen. When Pick noticed my presence, he stopped and climbed off the bed.

"Just gonna change." he smiled.

Before Josie's fog could clear, I was over to that bed and hoping on it. "How you doin', sweetheart?" I asked and lay down on the side closest to the door.

She didn't answer, too in the zone. Her body was controlling what she was feeling. So instead, she reached for me, her arm curving around my neck and pulling me down so our lips met. She kissed me and again my dick was hard in seconds. It wanted in her, but I had bad news for him because we weren't going there. This was about pleasuring her and nothing more. I'd already got off that night. It was Josie's turn.

The bed dipped on Josie's other side, letting me know Pick was back. I looked up to see he was also only wearing a pair of black boxers.

"Precious," he said. I shifted back so she could turn to him. "Are you wet, baby?"

"Y-yes," she stuttered.

"Can I feel?"

Christ. Yes.

"I-I... "

"It's okay, sweetheart. If you don't like it or anythin' in any way, just let us know, yeah?"

She nodded slowly. I sent a chin lift to Pick before my lips went to her neck. She arched for me and while she was distracted by feeling my lips upon her, I lifted her tee up past her stomach and chest. Her handful of breasts were covered in her red lacy see-through bra. My dick jerked under my boxers because as I gently smothered her in kisses, I watched her boobs rise and fall rapidly. Red was my favourite colour on her pale skin.

Josie tilted her head back, her eyes closed tightly. I watched as Pick kissed her stomach and then his fingers trailed up her thigh still covered by her jeans. I stared intently as he undid her button and slowly slid down the zipper, all while I kept her mind from going there with my lips, tongue and teeth. Once he had the zipper all the way down, he looked up and met my gaze. Fuck, we were both excited about this part. I could see Pick's erection pressing against his boxers like mine was.

Moving my lips down to her chest, just above her breast, so I could watch more closely. Pick licked his lips. Yeah, fucker, I wanted a taste of her as well. His hand slowly slid between the gap her jeans made... and that was when she froze.

CHAPTER ELEVEN

PICK

*D*ammit. Her mind had just caught up with her body. As soon as I felt her body tense up when my fingers touched the outer part of her soaked pussy's lips, I removed them. Billy went up to his elbows to look down at her. She had a hand flung over her eyes. Before we got the chance to say anything, she moved, scooting up the bed until her back hit the headboard.

"I-I'm sorry, so sorry." Her words were laced with sadness.

Eli moved up next to her where I stayed halfway down, only getting to my knees. "Why're you sorry, sweetheart?" Eli asked gently.

"I ruined it."

"No, babe, you didn't." He smiled down at her and took

her hand. "Could you, maybe tell us what happened in that beautiful head of yours?"

With her free hand, she quickly pulled down her tee and then placed her hand over her eyes, while she shook her head back and forth. Fuck, her bottom lip trembled, I wanted to punch a fucking dead guy for fucking her mind up.

"Precious, you're safe with us and, baby, you can tell us anythin'." I laid a hand on her bare foot. She flinched.

Clenching my jaw before I yelled the house down, I moved my hand away from her. She shifted her hand away from her face. Her eyes wide as she reached out to me, and I took her outstretched hand in mine.

"I-I'm sorry. I didn't mean to flinch. I'm sorry. Goodness, I'm so sorry. I enjoyed everything that was happening, but then my mind took me back *there*. It took me to *that* room." Her hand went over her mouth.

"Sweetheart. What happened in that room? Babe, we need to know so we don't do somethin' that will freak you out again," Eli asked.

She nodded her understanding, only said nothing. She looked from me to Billy and back again. Then her eyes glanced over the bedding. She sucked in a breath. "He would come in and he would... he did things to me. He would... he'd say nothing except—" She bit down hard on her bottom lip to keep it from trembling. Billy dropped her hand to move his to her mouth. She let up biting as he ran his thumb over her lip again and again.

She smiled sadly up at him and then her eyes went back

to the bed. Was she ashamed to look at us when she spoke of her fucked-up times? She shouldn't feel the need to hide her gorgeous eyes from us. We needed her to know that.

"I had to call him daddy when… when he was in me. Every time he'd roughly put his… um, his fingers in me and then he'd rip my clothes from my body and take me."

"Motherfuckin' cunt," Billy hissed.

Glaring at Billy to control his wayward anger, he gave me a nod. Even though on the inside fury blazed a trail through my own veins. His nostrils flared again and again. I knew what he was thinking, because I was thinking the same thing. We wanted a chance to kill the fucker again. At least his life was snubbed out by my own hands.

"Sweetheart, what… what he did will never happen with us. When Pick put his hands down your pants, did that set you off?"

She nodded.

Christ. I'd made her go back there. *I* caused it and that gutted me.

With what I'd been through, I should have known better. We should have talked before anything like that happened. But we were caught up in the moment and hell, I never would have thought something like seeing Billy and me together like that would have started it. At the time, all I could think about was Billy's body getting me off and then to know Josie, our girl, was watching us and liking it… I was crazed to please her in that way, by just having her watch us.

Fuck, I was the one to bring back her hell.

My hand fell from hers and I went to climb off the bed. I couldn't take being in there knowing I brought back the memory of her abuser.

"Caden," Josie cried out. I turned to face her. All of her fear disappeared as she glared at me. Instead, she was pissed about something. I would have laughed if I wasn't feeling sorry for myself. "Don't you dare leave."

"Baby, it's okay. I should have known better. We should have talked through the things that could set you off before jumpin' the gun and doin' it." I wiped my hand down my face. "You need some rest. Billy should stay in here for the night with you, precious. In case... hell, in case any nightmares come from what I'd done."

"No!" she snapped and got to her knees. "I-ah, okay, I'm going to say this." Her cheeks tinted pink. "I liked what was going on. I... I wanted something more to happen. I-I still do, I'm not used to feeling my body react like that. But, um, maybe... I don't know, maybe I could remove my clothes first?"

Holy shit.

Billy's head shot to me. Mine to him and we stared at each other. Had we heard right?

"I don't want *him*," she snarled with her lip raised and all, fuck it was cute, "to come between the three of us."

"But, sweetheart—" Billy started.

"No, please. Please don't stop this from happening."

"I don't think we should—" I began.

However, no matter what I was about to say, Josie wasn't

going to listen. To prove her point, she whipped her tee from her body and threw it to the floor.

"Ah… " Billy started and then snapped his mouth shut when she stood on the bed and slid her jeans down her legs.

"There," she stated happily with her hands on her hips. "Now my mind can't freak out… but, um, is, ah would it be okay if I left my panties on?"

I threw my hands in the air and shook my head. "Sure." I was at a loss for words. Josie stood in front of us in red lacy see-fuckin'-through panties and bra.

Nope, there went her bra.

"Wow." She smiled. "I've never felt so… "

"Sexy?" Billy growled.

"Gorgeous?" I offered with a smirk because there was our shy, sweet Josie standing before us in nothing but panties. *Did I mention they were see-through?*

"No, but thank you." She blushed and sat on the bed, her legs crossed in front of her and I wanted to rip them apart to take in her scent. "I was going to say freeing. Maybe I should walk around virtually naked more often."

Fucking Billy, his hand shot straight up in the air. "I agree," he yelled. "As long as no one else sees you," he added, I nodded in agreement.

"Okay then," she teased. Her gaze swung to me and then I was a goner. "Caden, please come back to bed." If her blush didn't deepen and dip to her chest, I would have sworn our girl wasn't embarrassed by letting her inner minx out.

"Hell yeah." I grinned and crawled on to the bed at the end. "Are you sure—"

She interrupted with, "I promise to let you know if something's happening up here." She touched her finger to her temple.

Nodding, I looked to Billy who was still leaning against the headboard and then to Josie. "Go sit on Billy's lap, baby." Billy looked at me with a question in his eyes, but I ignored it. Hopefully, my plan would work, and our girl will find her mind too occupied to go anywhere unwanted.

Josie pushed her hair from her face and then to one shoulder. I waited to see if she would listen and then winked at her when she started to move. She got to her knees and knee walked toward an eager looking Billy.

"Come here, sweetheart." Billy smiled, his arms wide and legs straight out on front of himself. Josie giggled and sat sideways on his legs. His arms surrounded her waist and he kissed her temple then neck. He palmed her naked breasts and she wiggled on his lap. I was sure he'd be back to having a hard-on with the way she was moving on his groin.

However, I wanted to join in on the fun as well. "Josie," I said.

"Hmm," was her response because already she was back to feeling what Billy's mouth was doing to her.

"Baby, face my way," I ordered with a gruff voice.

Billy looked up, so her head turned toward me. "Move around and face me, precious."

She nodded and shifted around, her legs went to either side of Billy's.

"Eli," she gasped.

"Yeah, sweetheart, you're makin' me so fuckin' hard," he

groaned and bit down on her shoulder. Through hooded eyes, she looked up at me and smiled. I just bet she was wondering what was going to happen next.

She didn't have to wonder for long. I crept up closer on my knees. "Bend your legs, baby and put your feet to the bed."

"Christ, yes." Billy grinned. He knew what I was up to.

She hesitated for a second and then bent her knees, spreading her legs more, to each side of Billy's legs. Her pussy was on full view now and I could see through the lace she was drenched.

Josie leaned her head back against Billy's shoulder while both his hands toyed with each breast. She was a tit girl, loving the caresses, and could probably get off from having her tits played with.

"Baby, you're so wet for us," I hissed. "I'm gonna touch you there, okay? It's just us here, precious, no need to be scared. But if you don't like anything I'm doin', just say so, yeah?"

"Y-yes, Caden." Fuck, her voice dripped in lust.

Leaning forward on my knees with one hand to the bed, I gently and slowly cupped her sex. "So hot, baby, so hot and beautiful." When she didn't freak, I applied more pressure to two fingers and rubbed harder against her.

"Oh," she panted, closing her eyes. "T-that feels nice... I-I've never felt that before down there."

Christ, did the fuckhead do nothing for her but get off himself?

Billy, wondering the same thing, asked, "Sweetheart, you ever touched yourself down there and came from it?"

"Huh?"

Billy met my gaze. Her answer was enough. Mother-fucking Christ, she'd never come before. Ever.

My male pride wanted me to pound against my chest at the thought I was going to be the first one to make her climax.

"Babe," Billy growled in her ear as he tweaked her nipples causing her hips to grind down and up. "We're gonna make you feel so good."

"Yes," she whispered.

"Precious, I need to move your panties aside, but you'll keep them on, is that okay?"

"Uh-huh," she said with a nod.

Licking my lips, finding myself so fucking keen to taste her, I reached to the side of her panties and tugged them over. She still had her eyes closed, so I wanted to surprise her with my next move. Moving my knees apart to each side of Billy's feet, I got to my elbows and then leaned in. First, while Billy watched, I drew in her scent.

Fuck. She smelt delicious.

Testing, I stuck out my tongue and took my first lick from bottom to top. Her eyes sprung open and stared down at me.

"Caden," she whispered unsure.

"Just relax, sweetheart, and feel it," Billy encouraged.

While keeping her gaze, I leaned in again and tongued

her clit. She nearly jumped off Billy's lap, but he had a hold of her.

"I, oh, ah." She didn't know what to say.

Again, I went back to her clit and wiggled my tongue against it. She squirmed on Billy's lap and from the way his head was thrown back against the headboard, her arse was rubbing his dick the right way.

Her scent was getting to me, driving me crazy, and I wanted more.

So I took it.

I sucked, nipped and tongued up and down, side to side, all while she panted and fucked my face. When her hand slid into my hair and pushed down, I groaned against her and she let out a mew of sounds. My hand slid into my boxers and I palmed my dick. I was that fucking hard it wasn't going to take me long to come.

"Caden, oh, God, Eli. Something… stop, something's happening to me."

I couldn't stop. I didn't want to. I wanted her to have her pleasure, to feel her release.

Thank fuck Billy wanted it as well. "Just go with it, Josie. Come on his face. Look at him, babe. He wants it. Just let it go. Ah, shit, babe, you're gonna make me come again from the way you're movin' over my dick. Yeah, sweetheart, like that, ah, yeah, Josie. Let him eat you out while I watch. Fuck, shit. I'm gonna come. Keep movin' just like that, yeah… fuck yeah, babe." Billy grunted through his release and I groaned as my hand pumped out mine into my boxers.

Josie stilled and then her back arched. "C-Caden," she

cried and forced my head harder onto her pussy. As soon as I slid two fingers inside, her walls clenched down around them milking my fingers as I took my last few licks.

Josie slumped back against Billy looking sedated. I wiped across my mouth with the back of my hand before I leaned forward to touch my lips against hers.

She slowly blinked her eyes open. Her hand reached up to cup my cheek. "I think I've been missing out on a lot."

Billy and I chuckled. "Yeah, precious, but now you have us."

Billy ran his hands over her stomach and sides before adding, "Anytime you wanna free the tension from your body, Pick and I are more than willin'."

She giggled and then yawned behind her hand. "Our girl needs some sleep," I said.

"Hmm," she uttered, her eyes already drooping.

Billy slid her off him and she curled to her side. "Love you, guys," she mumbled. Even though I didn't think she knew what she just said, we heard it and we fucking loved it. My chest warmed. I wanted to reach out and take her into my arms. I wanted to slide my dick into heaven... but not yet. Billy got up from the bed, his eyes soft on our woman. Her words had also affected him. "I'm gonna clean up and crash in Parker's bed. You sleep next to her tonight."

My head went back. "You sure... we could all fit."

"Nah, man. I'll take her bed tomorrow night. Don't want to crowd her in case she... "

Got fucked-up dreams.

"Good thinkin', brother. S'all cool with me, whatever you

135

want." And I honestly meant that. We worked well together, I was looking forward to seeing what the future would bring.

After I cleaned myself up again, I went back into Josie's bedroom. She was already deeply asleep. When I climbed in behind her, shifting her so the blanket was over us instead of under her, she stayed asleep. I curled my arm around her waist and even in her sleep she snuggled her back into me.

Yeah. My future was definitely looking up. If anything came to ruin it, fuck it up, there'd be hell to pay.

CHAPTER TWELVE

JOSIE

a warm, heavy weight was across my waist when I woke. Holding my breath, I started to feel panic, until I slowly glanced behind me to find Caden's sleeping form. My whole body sagged in relief and then thoughts of last night flooded my memory.

Goodness.

I'd fallen asleep right after…

My cheeks heated.

No one's head had been down *there*. No one. And the way Caden and Eli made me feel was like nothing I had ever felt in my whole life. I wanted to feel that again and again and again.

They cherished my body. The way their hands, mouths, skin felt against or on mine was beautifully erotic.

Goodness. Heat bloomed in the pit of my stomach at the thought. I wanted that tingling feeling to intensify like it had last night.

I wonder...

Could I touch myself down there and do what I had to do before Caden woke?

I wasn't sure, but my body wanted me to have a go. Moving my hand from Caden's arm, I drifted it down slowly so I wouldn't startle Caden awake. I was still in my panties, so I slid my hand under and was so close to touching that Caden's voice piercing the quiet room made me jump.

"Precious, let me take care of you," was growled behind me.

My heart nearly beat out of my chest. My stilled hand trembled when I felt Caden's arm move from my waist and down straight into my panties where my hand was still frozen.

"Baby, you want me to make you feel good?" he whispered sleepily and then... oh Goodness, he bucked forward and I felt his penis was already hard. "Let me take care of you, precious."

My mouth was too dry to speak. I only hoped he felt me nod. I guessed he did when his hand gently removed mine and then dipped back in under my panties to glide two fingers up and down my opening.

"Spread 'em for me, honey." His voice was thick with desire. Did a man really like doing that sort of thing to women? I mean, did they enjoy it so much they got aroused themselves? I never understood what got them horny, but I was starting to understand it more.

When I didn't move fast enough, Caden nudged his knee between my legs and then I lifted my leg up and over Caden's. I was rewarded by having his fingers slide in deep through my wetness.

"Fuckin' beautiful," he groaned and as his fingers glided in and out of me, I pushed back on his hardness. He seemed to enjoy that a lot. I could tell by his grunted response and how he rubbed his erection against me with more enthusiasm.

However, when his thumb pressed down, then up and over my nub, my mind blanked. I arched and turned my head. I wanted his mouth kissing me. Caden, understanding my need, got to his elbow, leaned over and claimed my mouth with his. He forced his other arm under me to hold me tight against him as he ground his erection into my arse and fucked me with his fingers.

His mouth moved from mine and kissed my cheek before whispering in my ear, "You like that, baby? My fingers fuckin' your perfect pussy?"

"Y-yes, Caden."

"Yeah, baby, look at you ridin' my fingers. Fuckin' glorious."

"Oh, God, it's happening again," I cried.

"Let it go, baby, let it go." And I did. My walls squeezed Caden's fingers tightly inside of me and my juices flowed out.

Caden kissed my neck, my shoulder and then lips. "Beautiful, fuckin' beautiful," he growled. "Baby... "

"Yes, Caden?" I breathed, still coming down from the molten feeling of ecstasy.

"You, ah, you mind if I finish off? Or I'll go to the shower and do it."

Rolling over as quick as I could, I looked up at his smirking face and asked, "Do you mean coming?"

He tucked my hair behind my ear and smiled. "Yeah, precious."

"C-can I watch?"

"You can help, if you want."

I grinned and he saw it, making him chuckle. "Yes, please," I begged.

"So sweet and beautiful," he uttered against my lips before rolling to his back and pulling his erection free of his boxers.

"What do I do?"

"Have you ever given a hand job?"

Biting my bottom lip, I shook my head and then blushed. That was why I was frightened, convinced my inexperience in the bedroom would bugger everything up. I hardly knew a thing. All David taught me was to lay there and call him daddy.

"S'okay, baby. I like that you haven't. It's another thing Billy and I can teach you, 'cause not all blokes like it the same way."

With courage, I reached out my fingers and ran them over Caden's stomach. His chest was full of tattoos, but his stomach was bare. I enjoyed the way it dipped or quivered from my touch. "So, Eli won't like it the same?"

"He could, not sure, baby, you'd have to try it with him."

"Okay, I will." I nodded. "After this though."

Caden burst out laughing. "Our little minx is so eager now. But you'll have to wait until later. I heard the front door earlier, means Billy's gone out for a run." He smiled at my sour face to running and not having Eli in the house. "Now, baby, I want you to wrap your hand around my dick."

"Like you have?" I asked and he nodded. I would have done what he asked, but I was rather liking the way his own hand slid up and down his erection.

"You like to watch me handle myself, precious?"

"Yes, very much so."

"Ah, honey, I'm glad and any other time, I'd put on a show for you. But, baby, I'm close to comin' already. I want to feel your hand on me."

Straight away, I reached out. I wanted to be the one to drive Caden to his last moment. Curling my hand around his warm penis was a strange sensation. I never thought it would be so warm and hard, yet still soft, in a way. I liked the feel of Caden. It made me wonder what it would feel like inside of me.

"Baby," Caden groaned in frustration. "You can stare at him all you like, but I need you to move your hand up and down on him." I started and again, I found myself enjoying what I was doing. From the hooded look in Caden's eyes, the way sweat beaded his brow and especially the way he moved his hips up and down to my hand action, he was getting off on what *I* was doing to him. "Yes, Josie, fuck, just like that. Feels so good, baby," he growled.

Goodness, just watching him was turning me on again. My clit throbbed. It wanted some attention. Watching Caden was the sexiest thing I had ever seen.

"Fuck, baby, I'm gonna come," he moaned. The muscle in his neck tightened. His head flew back into the pillow and he cried out through his release. I watched his face and then when I felt wetness on my hand, I looked down to see his semen ejaculated over his stomach.

I could have come myself easily with a little tweaking.

Rubbing my thighs together didn't help the way my pussy was pulsating.

"Caden," I whispered before kissing his cheek.

He chuckled. "Precious, I would love to take care of you again, but I've never come that hard. How about you wait for Eli to come home? I know he'd be more than willing to ease your ache, baby."

"Oh no," I moaned.

"What?" he asked and then leaned over to my bedside table where a box of tissues were. He moved back to his back and started to wipe himself clean. "Jose, you gonna let go of him now?"

"Oh," I gasped. I hadn't realised I still had a hold of his penis. "Sorry." I blushed.

Caden laughed. "Nothin' to be sorry for. I'm glad you didn't want to let go. Shows me you just enjoyed yourself."

"I did. I really did."

"Now, what was wrong then?"

"I just realised I have classes to get to, so I won't see Eli until this afternoon."

Caden again burst out laughing and then curled on top of me. "Baby, it'll make Eli's day hearing you're all pouty for not being able to get a taste of him this morning, but the anticipation will make it so much better."

"It will?"

He kissed me deeply before he pulled back and said, "Oh, yeah. Now let's get up, get ready and go."

"Okay then." I smiled.

I had a feeling that the day would be a good one.

ELI

By the time I'd come back from my run, Pick and Josie were already gone. The run took me longer because I was trying to outrun my erection. I needed it to settle the fuck down. Didn't fucking work. What didn't help was hearing Caden pleasing Josie before I left. I badly wanted to go in and join them... then again, I also wanted them to have their own fun, just like I prayed I'd get to have time with our girl by myself.

My dick wasn't happy about my decision. I was sure he'd even be happy to have Pick's body on me again because, Christ, I enjoyed watching him come, getting my own release, and having Josie watch it all with rapt attention.

No, my dick was pissed when I didn't even rub one off in

the shower. Instead, I had a cold one, got out and dressed. I decided to go for a ride, see if there was anything I could help Memphis out with at the Caroline Springs charter. Like all Hawks compounds, there was also a mechanical business on the side of it. I was sure there'd be something for me to do there.

Pulling up into the car park out the front, I swung off my ride and stalked into the office. No one was at the desk, so I walked around it to the back working area.

"Yo, kid," Dodge called out. He knew I hated being called the kid as in Billy the Kid, but of course, the fucker still hadn't changed.

Instead of biting back, I sent him a chin lift before stopping in front of him. "What's goin' on?"

"Not much, man. Just gettin' the lay of the land."

"Anyone given' you trouble?" I asked while looking around the shed at some of the other Hawks members. Some I knew and trusted; however, there were many I didn't. Those fuckers would get a wakeup call soon.

"A few, nothin' we can't handle for now, until you and Pick the Dick get your arses here full time."

"Our woman comes first, you know that."

"Yeah, I get it. Fuckin' pussy whipped, like the rest of them."

"Best way to be." I grinned.

His brows rose and then he shook his head. "I'm still not seein' it."

"Wait 'til you find the right one."

His snort was loud. "I doubt that. No pussy is tyin' me

down. Hell, I still can't believe one pussy has got *two* of my brothers tagged. How you all manage it?"

"Ain't your fuckin' business."

Dodge held his stomach while he laughed heartily.

"Billy," I heard called. I turned to see Dallas standing just outside the coffee room. Dodge and I headed over that way.

"S'up, brother?"

Dallas Gan was still new to the club, but he came with a stamp of approval from Stoke and Mrs fucking Cliff. He was a quiet man, but still a mean motherfucker when the time came. I'd seen him once in a bar fight. Some idiots thought they could fuck around with Blue's brother, Jason, when he'd been visiting Ballarat. Two seconds. That was all it took for Dallas to knock the four of them out.

"Was this the guy givin' Jose trouble?" he asked and threw a paper on the table in front of me. Leaning over, I couldn't believe my goddamn eyes. There stood Cameron Peterson and he was standing behind his lawyer father. The mother was on Cameron's other side looking bored out of her brain. None of that I really cared about.

What I did care about was the fact I knew the fucker sitting it the chair at the front.

And I didn't like him one bit.

Worse, Pick would hate him even more.

I'd seen Cameron's father's photo once, and that was in Pick's room. The only thing changed about the fucker was his name. I'd seen the photo because Pick had it taped to his wall with six other photos.

They'd been the ones to abuse Pick when he was

younger. Pick had already hunted and killed five of them. The last was sitting in that photo with a smug smile. A smile I wanted to wipe off his face with my gun.

Wasn't my right though.

"That him?" Dallas barked again.

"Yeah, that's him."

"Want me to get rid of him, no trace and then you and Pick can stay clean for your girl?" Dodge offered.

"I'm more than happy to help," Dallas said.

I shook my head sadly. "You both know of Pick's past?"

"Yeah, brother," Dodge said.

"Yeah, was drunk with him one night. He said some shit that he probably doesn't remember. Fucked-up shit."

"Yeah, well, that guy there,"—I stabbed the paper with my finger to Cameron's father's face; his name written in black ink under the photo Nigel fucking Peterson—"he was one of those guys who fucked Pick up back in the day. I recognised the face, but the name is different."

Dodge whistled low. "Retribution?"

"'Course and it's Pick's right to bring it." Dallas smiled. "You brothers need help, call us."

"We will. May need someone to watch Josie for us while we pay the nice family a visit and tell Cameron here a few home truths about his daddy."

"Man, that's fucked up. But I love it." Dodge chuckled. "Let us know when, brother, and we'll be there."

With a chin lift of gratitude, I rolled up the paper and walked out. Pick and I were going to have a talk, and then we'd plan for some payback.

I WAS ALREADY HOME SITTING on the couch in jeans and nothing else when the front door opened and in walked a smiling Josie, followed by Pick, who was also grinning. Fuck, I didn't want to ruin his mood straight off. Not when it was the first time I'd seen him so fucking happy.

"Eli," Josie squeaked.

Raising my brows at her in question, wondering why she was suddenly nervous at seeing me, I said, "Hey, sweetheart. Have a good day?"

What in the fuck was going on?

She looked over her shoulder to Caden and then back to me and blushed. "Uh-huh. Um, I'll be back in a second," she said and then bolted down the hall to her room, closing the door behind her.

Again. What. The. Fuck?

I looked to Caden. He smirked and shrugged. "I'll go see her. No need to worry."

Worry? Hell, should I be? Christ, after what they shared that morning, were they going to tell me there was no room in their lives for a third?

Was I being shot down?

Got rid of?

Jesus, I hadn't thought of that option ever happening. The realisation hit hard and my heart burned at the possibility.

Leaning forward, resting my elbows on my knees, my head went into my hands.

Shit. Panic started to settle deep.

More people didn't want me.

Just like my fucked-up father and mother.

Where was I going to go?

How could I face Pick at the compound knowing he got what I'd dreamed of and wasn't willing to share… or was it Josie not willing?

Fucked if I knew.

No one was telling me crap.

"Billy, brother," Pick called, the couch depressed where he sat next to me.

"How long do I have before I have to leave?" I growled.

"What? No, fuck no. It's not like that, man. It would never be like that. Christ, you think I could take away your life from you, your home? Never, brother."

Sitting up, I turned to him. "Then what in the fuck was all that about?"

Pick chuckled. "She's nervous, but you'll see soon enough. By the way, she liked seein' you topless when she walked in."

My head flinched back in shock. "What?"

"Our girl is findin' her minx side."

"What do you mean?"

"Let's just say, it's lucky she has two men to keep her happy."

"I don't—"

"Shut it, she's comin'."

I sat back in the couch and waited for some fucking answers that apparently Josie was bringing herself. Pick got up and moved to the chair at the end of the couch. The whole situation was confusing as hell and I wanted to know what was going down. What I didn't expect was seeing Josie walk around the couch wearing different clothes from before. Earlier, she walked in wearing jeans and a tee. Now she was wearing a knee-length sexy skirt and a cami-top. Her hair was tied up in a ponytail.

"Hi, Eli," she said with a small, shy smile.

"Babe, come here and tell me what's goin' on." I held out my arm and straight away she moved to sit across my lap. Her feet up on the couch while her side was leaning into me. Already my chest eased. It was a good sign. She wasn't getting rid of me after all. Then what *was* going down?

One arm went around her waist at her back and the other I rested on her leg closest to me.

"So, you gonna tell me?" I asked.

Her cheeks tinged a dark red, fuck it was cute. Holy motherfucking Christ. Was what she wanted something sexual?

Jesus. Was that what Caden meant when he'd said she was coming into her minx side?

There was no chance I was going to control my dick now. Not when I had such sweet pussy sitting on my lap.

She squirmed on my lap, telling me she could feel my dick harden and I reckon she liked it a lot.

"What you need, sweetheart?"

"I, um…."

She may be coming into her minx side, but she was still as shy as anything, which was the cutest thing.

Looking to Caden, he winked and smiled. When she grabbed my hand on her leg, I turned back to Josie as she slowly slid my hand up her thigh. My heart beat fast as she slid it up under her skirt to her hot mound.

Surprise flickered over my features before I smiled wickedly at her and rubbed up and down. She hummed in response and I asked, "This what you need, babe, my hand on you?"

"Yes, please," she begged, her eyes half-mast.

Screw that, I wanted nothing between my hand and her pussy. "Sweetheart, lift your arse up. I wanna feel how wet and needy your pussy is with nothing between us."

Again, I was surprised she did lift up her arse, leaning her hands back against the armrest. With both my hands, I slid her panties down and threw them over to Pick. He grabbed them out of the air and smelled them.

"Fuck yeah." He groaned.

Christ, even I was turned on seeing him do it, so was Josie by the sweet sexy look on her face, a look full of desire. However, soon her eyes were back to me when my hand was under her skirt again, running up and down her entrance.

"Eli," she sighed.

"Lean back a bit, babe." She did and I slid two fingers inside of her, causing her back to arch and a moan to leave her sweet lips. "So fuckin' hot," I growled. "Lift your arse up, Josie, use your legs and fuck yourself with my fingers." Licking her lips, she lifted and went down on my fingers, then up again and again.

"Yes, yes, yes," she cried, she was so close to coming already.

Fortunately, I heard the keys in the lock and I was able to sit Josie back up on my legs, her skirt covering her lap before Simone came striding into the living room.

Simone stopped at the end of the couch, Josie had her back to her. She stood there smiling with her hands on her hips. "Hey, ya'll what's going on?"

Josie cleared her throat. "N-nothing," she stuttered. Then, as Simone went on to talk about her night with her new man and all about the movie they went to see, I glided my fingers up under Josie's legs. She tried to stop me, pressing her leg down on my hand, but I wasn't having it. My girl wanted her release. She was going to get it and learn how to be sneaky around people so she could still get what she wanted.

Lifting her legs up, so her knees were bent again, I leaned forward so there was no gap between us. Easy access. Her pussy was ready for the taking and I did. I watched Josie as she bit her bottom lip and slightly shook her head as I slid two fingers into her slick pussy. My thumb ran over her clit and she bit down on her bottom lip harder.

Our poor girl wanted to come and hard.

"Simone, you got a sec to show me the coffee maker in the kitchen?" Caden asked.

Simone looked around suspiciously with narrowed eyes. "Sure," she said and then thank fuck left.

"I'll keep her in there." Caden laughed.

"Thanks, brother, won't take long. Our girl is primed and ready." And I was so fucking hard.

As soon as I heard him talking to Simone, I wrapped my arm around Josie's back. Her head turned to me. She glared, but that left her face as soon as I touched my lips to hers and kissed the fuck out of her. Thumbing her clit and pumping my fingers into her heat, she moaned against my lips. It didn't take long before her walls clamped down on my fingers as she came quietly.

Withdrawing my fingers, I pulled them from under her skirt and licked them. Josie watched me, then melted against me, her arms going around my neck.

"What about you?" she asked in a soft voice.

"Don't worry about it. We'll deal with that tonight… my turn in your bed."

Moving back, she made my day by giving me a big smile and saying, "I can't wait."

Neither could I, but seriously I was going to have to rub one off before my dick and balls dropped off from all the blood that flowed into it. "Babe, you better go see your girl before she gets suspicious."

She gave me one last lingering kiss before she got up and went into the kitchen. I bolted for the bathroom. As soon as the door was closed, I leaned with one hand against the vanity and tugged my pants down. Next, I had my dick in my palm jerking off thinking of how hot our girl was when she came.

I didn't hear the bathroom door open or Pick slip in

until he cleared his throat. I let out a strangled cry and turned. "Fuckin' hell, Pick," I hissed.

He gestured with his chin to my junk. "Need a hand with that?"

My head jerked back, sending pain down my neck. "What?" I breathed.

He didn't say anything. Instead, he walked toward me, got to his fucking knees, shoved my hand out of the way and took my cock into his mouth.

His fucking mouth.

Hot, wet, and feeling fucking amazing, he slid my cock out to the tip and then all the way in again.

"Jesus," I hissed.

All control left me. I leaned my arse against the vanity watching as Pick sucked me off. "Faster," I growled and he did. He looked up at me with his hooded eyes and slid his mouth up and down my cock faster. I grabbed the back of his head and held him down on my cock, though giving him enough room if he wanted to escape. When he didn't move, I pumped my seed into his mouth. "Fuck, yes," I hissed when he sucked the last drop out of me.

Pick stood, his pants were undone, his hand palming his own cock. I flashed back to the drunken night when I last had his cock in my mouth. It'd been dark then, but fuck me, now the room was light and his dick was so fucking hard. He was close to coming. I could see it from the strain on his features.

Christ, he got off on giving me head... like I had that time with him.

Without thinking, I stepped up, my hand reaching for his dick and when it did, his hand fell away. He seemed confused by my actions, he glared down at me. Was he worried I'd stop? There was no chance of that happening.

Stepping up closer, so the front of my body touched his side, I jerked his cock off in my hand and met his glare, which was starting to thaw. I then leaned in and whispered on a growl, "You like my hand on you?" He didn't reply. His nod was all he gave me. I wasn't happy with that. "Tell me, *Caden*. You like my hand wrapped around your cock?"

"Yes," he snapped.

"Good," I said.

"But I want your mouth on me."

Pulling back to look at him, I raised a brow, "Really?"

"Yes," he said through clenched teeth. He was close to coming.

Smirking, I said, "All you had to do was ask." I got to my knees. My mouth opened and was around his tip, just in time for his cum to shoot out and hit the back of my throat.

I reckoned the three of us were going to work out just fine, and from the smirk on Pick's face, as we left the bathroom, he knew it as well.

CHAPTER THIRTEEN

PICK

The afternoon and night were spent in the apartment. I'd actually helped Josie out in the kitchen while Eli made some phone calls about some shit. Simone sat at the kitchen table teasing Josie about how she'd gone and made us all domesticated. Like that would ever actually fucking happen. There would be no way in hell I'd clean a house... unless Josie was doing it naked and needed some help with something.

Instead of biting back in a teasing way, I ignored her comments and eventually she gave up. So then she went on about how great the sex she had last night was. That got me to leave the kitchen in a hurry, thank fuck mostly everything was done.

As I walked out, Simone started cackling. I just bet she'd get along with Deanna real well.

It wasn't until a little later when I walked back in to grab a beer did I guess what Simone had been up to. From the blushing red cheeks Josie had going on, they'd been talking about bedroom shit. I couldn't help the chuckle that flew from my mouth. I walked past Simone, who was eyeing me up and down, to Josie.

Bending over, I gave her a quick kiss, before pulling back and stating, "I hope you're makin' us look good, precious."

"You bet your balls she is. Now I'm not only jealous, but I'm thinkin' of killin' her to take her place," Simone huffed.

Standing tall, I threw my head back and burst out laughing. Eli suddenly appeared in the doorway asking, "What's so funny?"

Wiping my eyes, I told him, "Josie's been talkin' us up to Simone. Now she wants to off Josie to get to us."

Billy smiled and walked to our woman. "Sorry, Simone," he said offhandedly. "But you touch our woman, there'd be hell to pay." He finished on a growl before he bent down and kissed Josie deeply. I grabbed a beer out of the fridge and leaned my arse against the bench, enjoying the show. Though, I could feel eyes on me, so I looked to Simone. She was watching and waiting for my reaction. Waiting for my jealousy to show. Well, she'd be waiting a fucking long time.

There wasn't any. Even when I knew they'd be sleeping in the same bed that night, I didn't feel an ounce of jealousy. Why? Because I knew they needed me as much as I needed them, and they cared for me as much as I did them.

What Billy and I shared in the bathroom earlier that day was proof enough we could all make it work.

As Billy nibbled Josie's neck, Simone stood from the table and yelled, "That's it! I'm going for a cold shower. Try to keep your hands off each other when I come back out." She was out of the room before Billy's lips left Josie's skin.

When he did pull back, however, Josie glared up at him. "That was rude… you and you,"—she pointed to the both of us—"make me forget my manners. We shouldn't do that with other people around."

"Baby." I laughed. "We're bikers. We're horny and we love to kiss you, touch you and we wanna do that shit in front of people, so we can show them *you* are ours."

"Oh." She blushed. "Well, maybe just keep it to a minimal."

Billy and I chuckled. Billy then went to the fridge to grab his own beer. Once he turned around, he said, "We need our own place."

"Good thinkin', brother."

"But, I can't leave Simone."

"Babe," Billy started. "If we find the perfect person to live here with Simone, would you move in with us?"

She licked her lips. A nervous tick I noticed she did a lot. "Um, isn't it too soon?"

Billy looked to me and then we both cracked up laughing.

"Hey," Josie scolded, standing from her chair at the table.

"Sorry, precious. But no, it ain't too soon. We've been waiting for you for nearly four years, and now we have you, we want to spend as much time as possible with just us. No interruptions, so we can have you in every room without anyone walkin' in."

"Oh, um… "

"Sweetheart, you want this, yeah, us?"

"Yes, of course." Her answer was instant. Fuck, I loved that.

Billy nodded and smiled. "Then I'll start lookin' for a place soon."

"Won't that be expensive? I only have a part-time job. I mean, after I graduate I'll hopefully get a better paying job being a social worker, but I'm not sure—"

"Baby," I interrupted. "You won't be payin' for anythin'. You're our woman. It's a man's job to take care of his woman."

She stood tall and snapped, "I won't be kept."

There was our minx with her backbone as well.

"Honey," Billy said gently. "You won't ever be kept. We'll all put in, but I can tell you now the way you put in will be different to us. Babe, we fuckin' suck at cookin', cleanin', hell any household chore, even shoppin'. We'd need you to do all that while we put in for the other household shit."

"That sound fair, Josie?" I asked.

She was thinking and I loved to watch her do it. Her head went to the side, her teeth worried her bottom lip and her eyes became unfocused.

Then, so fucking cute, her head snapped back up and she smiled. "Yes, that's fair."

"Great." Billy grinned and winked at her. "Now speakin' of food. I'm starved."

When we'd consumed dinner, after Simone came out of the shower looking flushed like she'd just knocked one off, we watched some TV. Only, it was getting late and I knew Josie had some classes in the morning before her shift at the diner. Simone had not long gone to bed. So I stood from the couch and announced I was hitting the hay.

Billy stiffened and then said to Josie, "Babe, get your cute arse to bed and I'll be there in a second. Just got to talk to Pick about some shit goin' on at the compound."

His words had me tense. That was until our woman came up to me for her goodnight kiss, and said, 'See you in the morning." She swayed her arse down the hall.

"Night, precious," I called. She turned, smiled, and waved before walking in her room and shutting the door.

Turning back to Billy he said, "Sit down, brother."

Fuck. I thought the day was good. I thought things were going great.

Did he regret what went down in the bathroom?

My arse hit the couch and I demanded, "What is it?"

He leaned forward and took something out of the back of his jeans pocket. He slid it across the coffee table. It looked like something from the newspaper.

"What's this?" I asked before picking it up.

"Brother, just look at it and you'll know."

Running a hand over my face, I knew this was going to fucking wreck my night. Picking up the clipping, I opened it and froze.

Fucking cunt. Stupid fucking cock-sucking cunt. He'd changed his name. That was why I couldn't find the bastard.

"Motherfucker," I whispered. My hand scrunched up the paper in my fist. I couldn't look at it any longer. "It's the fucker's father."

"Yeah," Billy uttered.

"You know who he is?" I hissed.

"Brother, I been in your room. I remember seein' the six people on your wall. All of them crossed out but that dick-head's face."

A stiff nod. "I'm goin' after him."

"Tomorrow. I have Dodge and Dallas comin' here to take Josie to uni and then work. We go to his office tomorrow."

"We?"

"Yeah, brother, we. I got your back, man."

"His office isn't a good place if the man ends up disappearin'. People will ask too many questions."

"I have an idea about somethin', but it means the guy livin' for a little bit longer."

"Tell me," I growled.

"I've got Cameron's number in my phone. We call him, get him to meet us at his dad's office. Got a deal to make. Nigel gets Cameron to stay away from our woman or else you go public with the shit he did. We also get to tell Cameron just what kinda dad he has." He pauses to get my reaction. It was fucking brilliant. A smile lit my face as he continued, "Then, give it time, we take Nigel out."

"He needs to stop breathin'," I snapped.

"And he will," Billy stated.

"By my hands," I vowed.

"Done."

"Make the call and get to bed. You got beauty waitin' for you," I said and stood from the couch.

"Brother, you need to sleep easy, you take the bed."

"'Preciate the offer, but I'd be shit company tonight and Josie will sense somethin' is up. I ain't ready for questions."

"Pick, she knows about your past."

"Yeah, but she doesn't need to know I'll be killin' the last fucker soon."

Billy sighed loudly. "As long as you're sure."

"I am. Night, Eli," I said quietly and walked off to the hall.

"Night, Cade."

That actually made me smile.

Even when my past just surfaced, I still grinned because I had two people in it worth smiling for.

ELI

Josie was asleep when I got in the bedroom. Not that I minded. Watching her sleep was surreal. It was like I was imagining such a beauty in a bed I was about to climb in. Her fiery hair was splayed out on the pillow. She was on her side facing my way, her hands tucked up under her cheeks.

Fuck. She was heaven.

I felt like a prick though, as I was in there with her when I thought Caden could do with her sweetness, her closeness.

Then again, I knew where his head would be, and he was right. He wasn't in the right place to be next to innocence. Even though Josie lost the choice of giving her body freely, she still had an innocent air surrounding her.

Pulling the tee over my head, the one I put on when we were eating dinner, I threw it to the floor and then shuffled out of my jeans, leaving my boxers on. I gently shifted the blanket back and climbed in. Josie seemed to be totally out of it. I scooted over closer to her, facing her. My arm rested on her naked waist.

Wait, naked?

Holy shit. What was she wearing?

Of course, being a male, I had to take a look. I lifted the blanket up to take a peek and found our girl in panties and a sports bra.

Jesus, she was trying to kill me with her perfect body.

Groaning, I let the blanket drop. Now my dick was perking up thinking it was time to play. *Down boy, down, not yet you mongrel.*

I ran a hand over my face and then to the back of my neck. *Think of something else, anything else but about the glorious warm body next to you.*

I forced myself to focus on Cameron and the phone call I made before bed. It was easy. He'd picked up after the second ring, answering with a chirpy, "Hello." Then, he fell silent when I told him who it was and what I wanted him to do. He said he had an appointment with his dad tomorrow for lunch. Caden and I arranged to meet them at the restaurant across the way from his father's firm.

I couldn't fucking wait. What I also couldn't wait for was the time to come for Caden to get his retribution.

Hell, when Caden said my name earlier, instead of my biker name, it made me realise the strength of the connection between us. Not only because of Josie, but because I'd always thought of him as more than just a brother.

Christ, I needed to get to sleep instead of sounding like a fucking pussy.

Eventually, I did, curled around our sleeping woman.

FIRST THING I felt waking was a hand roaming around my stomach when I woke. I peeked through my eyes to see it was still dark outside. What the time was, I had no clue. But that hand suddenly seemed very eager and then so was the voice that came next.

"Eli," Josie whispered with a plea in her voice.

"Babe?" I asked groggily. "What's wrong?"

"I-I woke up… " I heard her moisten her lips. She was nervous.

"Sweetheart, you should know by now you can tell me anythin'." I moved her enough to get my arm around her shoulders. She rested her head on my chest, her hand still gliding across, up and down my stomach. "You have a bad dream?"

"No. I… since you and Caden have been here, the night-mares have gone."

Hearing that was gold.

"I'm glad, babe. So what's up?"

"I was wondering… can I, would you mind if I, um… touched you?"

My body stilled. Holy hell, had I heard our girl right?

Now it was my turn to lick my lips. "Josie, you mean you wanna touch my cock?"

She hid her face into my chest more, and then whispered the most magical word, "Yes."

I took her hand in mine and slowly led it from my stomach down to my boxers and ran her hand over my dick. "You mean like this?" I queried.

"Mhmm," she mumbled with a nod. "But, also without the boxers in the way."

"Jesus, woman, you're killin' me here." I took my hand from hers and pushed down my boxers letting my hard cock bounce back on my stomach. "Touch me, sweetheart," I growled, leaving my hands down at my side.

Her touch was light at first, until she took hold of my dick in a firm grip and started to slide her small hand up and down my length.

"That feels so good, Josie. So fuckin' good." Her rhythm picked up and if she wasn't careful, I was going to embar-rass myself and come soon. Her body started moving beside me, squirming. Christ, she was getting turned on from touching me. Her legs rubbed together over and over as she kept up the motion on my cock with her hand.

"Eli," she whispered into the dark room.

Crap. It wasn't the time for a conversation. I was about to blow my load.

"Yeah, ah, fuck, yeah," I groaned when she ran her thumb over the tip of my nob.

"Eli, I really need something."

"Tell me," I asked on a growl. If she wanted anything, I would give it to her.

"I would like,"—she squeezed my cock—"this inside me."

Shaking my head, I thought, again, that I was hearing things… or was I dreaming?

"Please?" she begged in a soft voice.

"Sweetheart, you sure?"

"Yes."

"Ah, I-I… " Crap, I was stuttering. "Do you want Pick in here as well?"

She ran her hand up my stomach, letting go of my cock before she said, "Do you think he should be?"

"Maybe." Honestly, I was leaning toward yes. I knew what I'd want in that situation. If it were Josie's first time with one of us, I'd want to be there to see it and watch her through it. "Yes," I said and quickly climbed out of the bed, turning on the bedside light. "Be back in a tick." I smiled over my shoulder while pulling my boxers back up. Opening the door, I stepped out, praying I didn't run into Simone. We really needed a place to ourselves. I walked down the hall and without knocking, I opened the door to Pick.

Already knowing he probably wasn't sleeping, I found

him sitting on the bed, already in boxers while thumbing through his pictures on his phone. Probably looking at the ones we'd taken with Josie over the last month or so.

Stepping in, I closed the door behind me. Caden sat up quickly. "She okay?"

"Yeah, brother. But, ah, fuck. Okay she wants to fuck."

He blinked slowly and then hissed, "Say what now?"

"She wants to have sex, now. We thought you'd wanna be there for it."

"Fuck, yes." Caden grinned and got off the bed. He had the door open in a second and was back in Josie's room in the next second. Hell, I wasn't far behind.

"Caden," I heard Josie say and I just fucking knew it'd be with a smile.

"Shift over to the middle, precious," Caden ordered.

Once she was situated and Caden had already hopped in beside her, I quickly followed suit. On my side, up on my elbow, I looked down at Josie to see her cheeks red like her hair. "Babe, we need to know, you on the pill?"

"Yes."

"I'm clean," I provided and looked to Caden.

"Hey, you're running the show. I'm just here to watch. But if you wanna fuckin' know, I'm clean also."

"Now we got that out… " I grinned down at Josie.

"Are we going to turn off the light?" Josie asked.

"Hell no, baby," Caden said. "We wanna see you. But you okay with that?"

"I think so," she said with a shy smile.

"You ain't, you tell us, yeah?" She nodded. "Caden, how

about you get her ready while I pay close attention to her mouth?"

"Sounds good to me." He smiled.

"Josie," I whispered. Her head turned to me and I claimed her lips with mine. My tongue came out to rub against her lips. She opened for me and touched her tongue with mine. Then, it got heated. She moaned against my lips as I thrust my cock against her hip. I opened my eyes enough to see Caden kissing her stomach while his fingers played with her bare pussy, panties no longer in sight.

Removing my mouth from hers, I trailed tender kisses down her neck, over her collarbone and to her chest. Then I pulled back and growled, "Pick, up here." I got to my knees and Pick moved up the bed to start kissing Josie. "Babe, spread," I ordered with a hand on her thigh.

Jesus, I was fucking excited to get inside her. It was like opening the best fucking Christmas present when you were a kid. I moved between her legs but sat back on my calves to watch Pick and Josie enjoying each other. Pick was playing with her bare tits and Josie, fuck, she had her hand down his boxers.

I didn't have to feel to know she was primed ready to go… but fuck, I was a guy, of course I still had to get my fingers on her sweet pussy. She jumped and tore her lips away from Caden when she felt the first gentle swipe of two fingers against her pussy lips. She was soaked.

"You want me inside you, babe?"

She bit her bottom lip and nodded.

"You want to stop, any-fuckin'-time at all, you tell me."

"Okay, Eli." She smiled shyly and there was her blush. I loved when her cheeks tinted for us.

Leaning down, I kissed her mound before kissing my way up her stomach to her breast. There I sucked in her erect nipple and gently applied pressure with my teeth. She moaned and grabbed the back of my head. However, I shook it off and leaned over her, my hands on the bed, my arms straight. "Spread further, sweetheart." She did. I took one hand off the bed and palmed my cock, lining it up with her, then thought better of it and rubbed the tip of my dick up and down, teasing her with it.

"Eli, please," she begged, her legs spreading further, wanting and waiting for me to enter.

Smirking up at her, she glared, got to her elbows so she could look down at us. She wasn't the only one though. A silent Caden, also got to one elbow and then hissed through clenched teeth when he saw I stopped playing and slowly started to push my way inside her fucking tight, wet pussy.

"You okay, Josie?" I asked even though it was a strain not to just pump all my cock inside her.

She looked from our bodies joining together up to me and smiled. "Yes, Eli." I slid in more and she moaned. "I'm more than all right," she said, flopping her upper half back down to the bed. "Th-that, it feels good. Better than good." Jesus, the way she was talking I couldn't help myself. I thrust all the way in. "Oh, God, more," she cried.

"Fuckin' beautiful," Caden voiced before he tore his eyes away from my cock now gliding in and out of Josie's soaked pussy, faster and faster, to me where he smiled. He then turned again to look down at Josie and his smile went bigger, brighter, when he saw her head thrown back in the moment.

"She feels, so good, Cade," I groaned.

"I bet she does. And she's ours."

"Fuck yes," I hissed low.

"Caden," Josie cried. "Kiss me, please." She didn't have to ask twice. Caden fell upon her lips with his own and ravaged them while I slid in and out of fucking heaven.

Shit. My balls were creeping up, I was going to blow my load soon, but I needed our girl to come first. I wanted to feel it all around my cock.

Lifting a hand from the bed, I pressed a thumb on her clit and moved it up and down twice before she exploded on a cry. Her mouth came away from Caden's. Her hands fisted the sheets and she brought her hips up to meet mine as her walls tightened around my cock, drawing the cum from my body.

"Ah, yes. Fuck," I yelled as my cum filled her sweet pussy.

Holy shit, she was still coming.

I pulled my cock free. Josie mewed her complaint at losing me, I growled at Caden, "Get up there, brother, she's still comin'."

Quickly, I moved out of the way, laying down next to Josie as her body shuddered and Caden climbed between her legs and thrust his cock straight inside her. She screamed out in ecstasy as Caden kept up his pursuit of pumping hard into her.

"Christ, the best, our girl is the fuckin' best," Caden barked deeply.

"Oh, yeah, brother." I smiled. "She stopped comin'?"

"Hell, no. She's so tight, so fuckin' beautiful."

"Oh, God, Eli… "

"Ride it out, babe, ride it out on Caden's cock."

"Yes," she yelled.

Caden groaned and then grunted. He stilled for a second before pumping faster and I knew he was coming. I knew the face he pulled when he came.

Both of them. Fucking beautiful, and mine.

Caden had no choice but to collapse down on top of Josie. He was exhausted just like I was, but especially our girl. Never had I seen a woman come that hard and long in my whole fucking life.

Caden rolled to her side. I watched his softening cock slip from her. At least I had a little more energy, so I leaned over the bed, picked up my tee and gently, knowing she'd still be sensitive, wiped our cum from between her legs.

"Hmm, thank you." Josie smiled with her eyes closed.

"Thank you, sweetheart, for trustin' us, for lettin' us in that gorgeous body," I said and then threw the soaked tee to the floor.

"Love you, guys," she said sleepily.

"Precious," Caden moaned and rolled into her, his arm going over her waist. "You're it for us. You're our home."

He held back from saying it, but what he said was enough for our Josie. She turned her head and kissed his lips before she turned to me. Against her lips, I whispered, "We love you, too, sweetheart, with all our fuckin' hearts."

She slowly blinked her eyes open and smiled brightly. "I have definitely been missing out on so much... but especially in the bedroom."

Both Caden and I chuckled.

"Lucky you have us now, baby," Caden said.

"And only ever us," I growled.

"Definitely." She smiled.

But seriously, right then, I felt like I was the luckiest one to have two people in my life I loved, who were willing to share their lives and love with me.

Not that I'd ever say anything to Caden. I was a mean motherfucker after all, and we didn't talk emotions and shit.

CHAPTER FOURTEEN

JOSIE

*S*omething was happening, but I had no clue what it was. Two weeks had passed and something was amiss with my guys. They were still very attentive to me. A smile slipped onto my lips at the thought. Yes, they were *very* attentive. However, I was getting tired of them mollycoddling me.

I knew I had to come in strong with a plan of attack to find out what they were hiding. They'd become very clever at distracting me with their bodies, and house hunting. Two days earlier, we had finally, after looking at ten different houses and apartments, decided on an already vacant three-bedroom weatherboard house. It reminded me of Mattie and Julian's house in Ballarat across from the compound. I even sent a photo of it to my parents. Mum loved it. Dad thought it was too old and needed some work. It was the next day, after classes I turned on my phone and found I had twenty-six messages. All were from my dad and most were pictures of certain types of tools my guys would need to fix our place up. The other pictures were of items of furniture. I'd looked through them all and then decided it was time to call my dad.

"Baby girl," he cried cheerfully into the phone when he picked up.

"Hi, Dad. Can you—"

"No time to talk, sweetheart. I'm at Ikea. I just found the perfect couch and chair set. They're bright green. What do you think of that?"

"Um—"

"Hmm, maybe not green, I just saw a blue set. Damn, yeah, they look better."

"Dad," I nearly yelled into the phone as I walked to my next class with Eli chuckling at my side.

"Yes, baby girl?"

"Why are you looking at furniture for us?"

"Well, because you'll need new stuff for your place with your guys. Your mum and I wanted to buy you somethin' for a house warmin' gift. She said a microwave or a vase, but that shit won't do for our baby girl. Don't you worry, I'll set somethin' up and get it shipped to you and then... you tell those boys of yours to have their crap ready. I'm comin' to stay for a while to help on the house."

Oh, goodness.

Even though I was scared of having my dad stay while I lived with two men, a smile slipped onto my lips, because my dad, no matter where or what age I was, never got tired of trying to take care of me.

So I sighed and said into the phone in a loving tone, "Okay, Dad. I'll let them know."

"Love you, baby girl," he said into the phone.

"Love you, Dad." I grinned before hanging up.

As an added bonus to the house, it wasn't far from Simone, the uni or the diner. Of course, I still had my reservations about moving in with them, especially when they were hiding something from me, something that was making them tense.

If it came down to it, I would have to decline the offer of living with them until they trusted I wasn't the timid, little girl they still saw in me. I wanted to be with them, with everything I was, and that also meant I would do anything for them. If in some way I could help them, I would. No matter the situation. No one was coming between my men and me.

I just had to show them I was a changed woman. I was stronger, and they had played the part to get me that way.

Yes, I may have been timid and a coward when it came to Cameron and his friends, but back then I felt I had nothing to care for.

I did now.

In fact, I had two.

And it was time they learned I was there for them and I'd risk everything for them.

"Darlin', sit the fuck down or you'll wear a hole in the carpet from all the pacin'." Dodge smiled from the couch.

"You got any fizz-pop?" Dallas called from the kitchen. That got me to stop pacing and turn to the direction of the kitchen. Did a bad arse biker just call soda a fizz-pop?

Fizz-pop.

"Woman?" Dallas called again and then his frame filled the doorway. "Fizz-pop, you got any at all?"

The giggle was untameable and once I started, I couldn't stop. My arm went around my stomach and I bent over laughing.

"What the fuck's up with her?" Dallas snapped.

"Probably hearing the word fizz-pop from your mouth."

Wiping my eyes, I looked up to see Dallas shrug and walk back into the kitchen mumbling, "I take that as a no. Bloody women are wacked."

"Darlin', good to see you smile and laugh. Now come sit next to Uncle Dodge and tell him what's goin' on in that head of yours."

Sighing, I went over to the couch and sat next to him. I was getting to know Dodge and Dallas more, after reuniting with them the morning after my first time with my men. Eli and Caden were sweet the next morning, hugging me and kissing me every chance they got. Though, while I was having breakfast, there had been a knock on the front door. After Caden answered it, he came back in with Dallas and Dodge. I hadn't been expecting to see them and when they said they were my men for the day, because mine had shit to do for the club, I accepted it without any drama. It had happened two more times since then and, even though I enjoyed Dodge's humour and Dallas's surliness, it still put me on edge, because, again, my men were keeping something from me.

"Dodge?" I started, wringing my hands together on my lap.

"Yeah?" he asked wearily.

"I know my guys are up to something, but it's something they're keeping from me and I'm starting to feel that it's something big. Also, I'm pretty sure it has nothing to do with club business else you and Dallas would also be there, and I'd be here with a prospect instead. So, my question to you is, do I need to be worried about my men?"

"Josie, you know I can't say shit. It's the brothers' code." *Stupid bloody code.* "Don't worry, darlin'. Don't get your panties in a twist about anythin'."

"Why're you talkin' about our girl's panties?" Eli glared from the front door.

I stood quickly and looked from Eli to behind him. "Where's Caden?"

Eli walked in and closed the door. I was in his arms after he took two strides my way. "Babe." He smiled before his lips touched mine. "He'll be up in a second. He's just on the phone with the realtor. They rang."

My eyes widened. My hands went to his chest and I pushed, stepping out of his arms.

Lie.

Eli had just lied to me.

"Big fuck up, brother." Dodge sighed.

"Josie?"

"Is it another woman? Do you both have some pieces on the side? I know I'm still learning, but I didn't think I was so bad for you both to seek it out somewhere else."

Wasn't that why lies started? The men were cheating? I'd heard stories about it happening all the time.

"Sweetheart, what are you fuckin' talkin' about?" He reached out.

I moved back again and then spun, walking even further behind the couch where I stood with my hands on my hips.

"Y-you just lied to me, Eli."

"What? No—"

"Brother, give it up," Dallas barked from the kitchen doorway. "Josie's spoken to the realtor. *They* just rang here."

"Fuck," Eli hissed. He turned his back on me and swore again. His hands ran through his messy hair.

Suddenly, the front door opened and in walked Caden. He looked from Eli to me and his already frowning face deepened. "What's goin' on?" he asked in an annoyed tone.

Eli sighed. "Our girl thinks we're steppin' out on her."

"What?" Caden barked.

"You've both been hiding something from me and Eli just lied to me. Who were you talking to downstairs, Caden?"

"The real—"

"Brother." Eli winced, shaking his head.

A snort left me. "Really, you as well? Fine. Just fucking fine," I yelled and stormed down to the bedroom, slamming the door behind me.

Swearing was something I never did, but at that time, it felt relevant and also very good. It matched my mood. Tears no longer threatened; instead, I was angry. Why would they choose to lie to me? I thought they wanted it all to work between the three of us. Had I been wrong?

Stupid men. They made my mind overreact on the cheating part. No, knowing them, they were probably trying to protect me from something. Didn't they see, with them at my side, I didn't need to be protected? If it had anything to do with them, I'd want to know, to help. I would want to be there for them.

But why were they not letting me?

Goddamn it. Why did it hurt so much when they lied?

If it were anyone else, I wouldn't care. I didn't trust many people like I did Caden and Eli, which was probably why having them lie to me hurt so much. It shredded my heart and put a dent in my trust for them. It made me want to scream and yet vomit. My insides were in turmoil.

PICK

Fucking hell, I'd gone from one nightmare to another. Only, the second one was worse because we'd hurt Josie. I never wanted that to happen, but I didn't want to involve her with what I'd learned.

The lunch date, two weeks earlier, went to plan... now it'd gone to shit.

We'd turned up on time to find Cameron and his fucked-up father already there, sitting in some crap pansy restaurant. They'd probably expected us not to make a scene. Little did they know that it would be Cameron making a scene.

Eli was in front when we walked in. We were both about the same size, so his view blocked me from the tables as the maître-d' quickly and quietly, after a disapproving look at both of us, led us to a table at the back.

"That's them, Father," Cameron said in a snotty tone.

I stepped around Eli and looked down at Nigel. I'd hoped he'd recognise me and freak the fuck out, but even after he looked at me from head to toe it didn't register who I was. Though, it had been fifteen years and I'd been just a boy when he violated me. The sick fuck took what he shouldn't have from me.

I was about to ruin his relationship with his prick of a son and I couldn't have been happier.

"Please take a seat and tell me why you have been harassing my son," he said with his nose turned up.

Shaking my head, I smirked and placed my hands on the table, leaning in. "We won't be staying, fuckhead. There is no way I would ever sit down with you."

His eyes widened. "Do I know you?"

A humourless chuckle left me. "I don't suppose you'd recognise me. It's been a very long time. First, I want you to listen and then do as I say or your life will be fucked up, even more than what it already is."

"You can't threaten me. I will call the police right now

and have you arrested," Nigel demanded. His son sat back in his chair and smiled smugly up at us.

Eli widened his stance and crossed his arms over his chest. Nigel flicked his gaze to Eli, narrowed his eyes on Eli's vest, and then looked back to me.

Smiling I asked, "You see that now, don't you? We belong to Hawks and your son here has been giving shit to one of ours."

Cameron snorted. "She's not one of yours. She's a club whore."

I felt Eli move. I glanced over my shoulder to see his hand going to his knife. I shook my head.

"Fuck," he hissed. "Make this quick then before I stab the fucker in the eye."

"Josie is not a club whore. She's our woman, and family to others in the club," I said to Cameron. He rolled his eyes. Looking to his dad, I added, "You get your son and his friends to stay the fuck away from Josie or we'll share some secrets of *your* past."

Nigel chuckled. "I have no secrets, so you don't have anything."

"You remember Rosemary and her kid?"

Fuck yes. I smiled.

Nigel paled and it was magnificent to see. He looked at me in new light, studied my face. "Y-your—"

"Yeah, cockhead. I'm the kid you sexually abused when I was only twelve."

He blanched and abruptly stood from the table. "What? I

don't have a clue what you're talking about. I would never—"

It was then I took a photo from my back pocket and slammed it on the table. Cameron was fast. I'd give him that. He snatched it up before his father got a hand on it. Watching Cameron studying the photo was fun. First, he screwed his nose up, then he gagged. His hand went to his upset stomach and then he stood just as fast as his father had and threw the photo at him.

"What, you didn't know your daddy was into little boys?" Eli taunted. "Did he leave his hands off you, Cammy?"

Cameron's eyes widened. Something triggered in his mind and I wondered what it was. His face turned glacial as he spat at his father's feet. "You disgust me. I never want anything to do with you again." He went to round the table.

Eli grabbed his arm. "Hold up there."

"You do as we say," I started. "Leave Josie alone and have your friends forget about her... or your father will have his past exploited in the newspaper. I'm sure you don't want everyone to know what your dad used to get up to when you were just a boy yourself. Everyone will think the same happened to you. You've always been supportive of your dad here. How would that look to all your friends?"

Cameron's hands fisted tightly. He wanted to punch me and all I could think was bring it. His face contorted with rage as he looked back at me.

"Cameron," Nigel started and placed his hand on his son's arm.

"Don't you ever fucking touch me," Cameron snarled before shaking off Eli's hold, after my nod to Eli, and stalking out of the restaurant.

"You better go after your son, Nigel. Don't want him to back out of the deal now." Eli smirked. Nigel quickly threw some money on the table and went after his son.

At the time we'd thought we'd won.

We were wrong.

It wasn't until two weeks later, early in the morning, when Eli got a call from Memphis telling him I had a delivery at the compound. Memphis was the president of Hawks in Caroline Springs, so we took orders from him. When he rang, we listened. He'd also said he'd sent Dodge and Dallas over to stay with Josie while Eli and I went to see what I'd received.

I'd left Josie warm in bed when Eli woke me quietly and gestured for me to follow him. After he told me what Memphis said, we were out the front in seconds, dressed and ready. Dodge and Dallas pulled up and went straight inside with a chin lift to us. Once we saw them through the door, we rode off.

Thankfully, the ride was only ten minutes because my mind was fucking with me on what it was and *why* in the fuck I would get a package sent to the compound.

Whatever it was, I knew it wasn't going to be good and I'd been right.

Eli told me Memphis would be waiting in the lunch room in the mechanical area. Brothers-in-arms were milling around working or talking shit. As soon as we were through the door to the lunch room, it closed behind us.

We turned and Eli had his gun pulled and aimed.

"Cool it, Billy," Memphis grumbled from his seat at the table.

"Dive, what in the fuck you doin' here, brother?"

Dive, a brother from Ballarat, grinned wide and came forward for a handshake and a slap on the back.

"Talon thought it'd be good for me to come. Apparently, the shit goin' down is worse."

Turning to Memphis, I glared. "What the fuck?"

Memphis rolled his eyes and sighed. "You got your own shit to handle. When it's over, you'll be in the full fold. For now, you got this to deal with." He slid a small rectangle box over the table and my stomach dropped when I saw the red trailing the box behind it.

Motherfucking Christ.

Whatever was in that box had bled.

"What the fuck?" Eli hissed.

"That's what we want to know," Dive said. "If this has anything to do with Josie, Talon's gonna—"

"We're protectin' her," Eli snapped.

"How?" Memphis demanded.

Eli looked to me and I nodded, he explained, "We already told you we dealt with the fuckheads hasslin' Josie. What we didn't tell you was how. The father of the main guy givin' shit to Josie was a man of Pick's past."

"What past?" Dive asked.

"Caden?" Eli uttered and fuck it to hell, it touched my

heart. I nodded again as I kept my gaze on the box.

"His mother used to sell his body to men and women. She also used to get him to do illegal shit so she could stay high or drunk. One of the guys who bought time with Caden is this Cameron's father. We approached them, told Cameron to leave Josie alone or else his father's past would surface and everyone would know."

"Do you have proof?" Memphis asked.

"Yeah," I said. Because I did. I had proof on them all. It was in the final week I'd decided enough was enough and I took footage of them all. Their faces were caught on camera when they... did things to me. I had that printed out into pictures, which was what Cameron had seen of his father.

"The dad's name, was it Nigel?" Dive asked.

My head snapped to him when he held out a note. "It was attached to the parcel."

"Jesus," I hissed before opening it to read.

Caden, or as your biker people call you, Pick.

You may have grown up to be a fine young man, but you will never be as cunning as I.

I have someone you may want alive. In the box is a piece of that someone and if you don't do as I SAY, then you will find more pieces of her turning up each day until you listen.

I want the whore.

You have forty-eight hours to say goodbye to the slut

and hand her over to Cameron where she works at 10 A.M. on Friday.

Nigel.

"Pick?" Memphis said. Tearing my eyes from the paper, I looked to him. He gestured with his head to the box. Fury, deep, unsettled fury burned inside of me. That fucker thought he could play with me again.

"No," I snarled. "I won't let the fucker have the satisfaction."

Whoever was in the box was going to have to stay there. I had no one worth worrying about except for Josie, Eli and my brothers. Fuck.

Jesus motherfuckin' Christ.

Had he taken a brother?

How?

No, it couldn't be. We would have heard.

"You need to know," Eli said gently. He picked up the box with a gloved hand and opened it.

Hell. Fucking hell.

"Do you know who…?"

Yeah, I fucking did.

I knew whose finger lay inside the small box.

My mother's. The ring her dealer gave her was still sitting on her dead finger.

Turning my back to them all, my hands ran again and again over my shaved head as I lifted my head and bellowed to the roof, "Fuck!"

CHAPTER FIFTEEN

ELI

*a*s I stared at Josie's retreating sexy form when she strode down the hall and then her bedroom door banged shut, I couldn't help but remember the conversation I'd had with Caden after he recognised the finger in the box. Josie didn't need to hear it, but unfortunately, we were running out of options after being caught out on a lie from both of us.

"Out," I'd growled to Memphis and Dive. Dive already had the door open and was out it before Memphis stood from the table and stalked around it. He took the back of my neck in a hold and pulled me in close. There he whispered into my ear, "Take care of our brother. Don't let him lose himself. If I'm guessin' right, it's his mother's finger. She ain't worth the trouble. Get him through it *and make the fuckers pay." With that, he left, closing the door behind him.*

"Caden," I started.

"You know who it is?" he asked with his back to me.

"Yes," I replied. "Come sit down, brother."

Caden snorted. "What, you gonna give me head to forget about that fuckhead cuttin' bits off of my mum?"

Angry. Of course he was. The man was playing him, and he didn't deserve it.

Like Memphis had done to me, I took the back of Caden's neck in my hand and steered him to the table, sitting him down in a seat. There I let go and sat next to him. His elbows went to the table and his head and eyes pinned to the box. So I picked it up, put the lid on it and threw it toward the trash can.

"Listen to me," I began, his eyes came to me and then returned to the table, telling me he was going to listen, but the clenched jaw told me he wasn't happy about it or the fucked-up situation. "Think back, Caden. Think back to how your own fuckin' mum used and abused you. Man, she gave an innocent boy's body to anyone who'd pay so she could get her fucked-up fix. She's never cared, Caden. If you go to her, help her, you will be sucked back into her nasty fuckin' web.

"Is she worth your time, your help when finally, fuckin' finally, Caden, you have pure beauty in your life? She'll ruin it, brother. She'll fuck up your life again." I placed my hand on his arm on the table. "Don't let her. She's usin' you again, usin' your heart to get what she wants. Don't let her win. She ain't worth it. You have us now. You have your own family and she is not a part

of it. The only good that woman did was give birth to you. Now she should be just a memory. Fuck, not even that, not after what she did to you. She's fuckin' nothin', Caden, not even worth a thought." I paused. "Let it go, brother. Let her go and move on to what comes next for you, Josie and me. Your family." I could only hope Caden would see reason with my words.

We sat in silence for a while. I watched him as his mind ran through many thoughts.

"I don't know if I could live with myself by just lettin' him have my mum."

"Are you willin' to hand Josie over for her?" I asked.

"Fuck no," he growled.

"Why'd you feel the need to save that bitch of a mother of yours? What's she ever done for you? Tell me of a fuckin' time she had your back and wasn't offerin' it up instead for her own life."

Nothing but silence.

Because there had never been a time his mother had his back.

Not like Hawks.

And not like Josie would.

"Fuck," he hissed. "Fuck!" he yelled. "She's nobody to me. I have no family but the brotherhood and... you and Josie."

"Damn right, Caden." I nodded. "Let's head home. Our girl will be wonderin' where we are."

Without another word, he stood and started for the door. Then he turned to me when I was a step behind him. He looked at me and gave me a half-smile. "Who knew we'd...? I 'preciate ya, man."

Grinning, I said, "Same."

On the ride home, I thought it was time to take the reins back into our hands. There was no way in fucking hell I was going to let the fucker ruin Caden's life. He had just started to live again.

I slid off my ride and waited for Caden to take off his helmet, I was about to tell him my plan when he spoke, "I'm gonna make a call to Lan. Maybe he can do somethin'. I can't,"—he shook his head—"I can't just let her die."

"You know what that means?"

"What?"

"You're the better man, outta any of 'em, us. Fuckin' always have been, you and Josie deserve each other, but I'm a selfish fucker and I'm taggin' along for the ride as well."

Caden threw his head back and laughed. "It wouldn't be the same without you, Eli. You fuckin' know that."

I sent him a chin lift. "'Cause I'm that awesome." I smirked. "Make the call, see you up there."

Looking to Caden after Josie stormed off, he stared back and then with a nod, he started for her bedroom door. He was going to tell her it all. I needed to be in there for them.

"Thanks for your help, brothers, but... "

Dodge chuckled as he stood from the couch. "Yeah, yeah we get it. Make-up sex and truth work wonders."

A snort, then a shrug. "True that," I said.

Dallas walked to the door from the kitchen. "She's strong now. She can handle it." He glared and then left. Dodge sent a wink before he closed the door after him.

Dallas was a strange fucker and the woman who brought him to his knees was going to have to be the sane one for the both of them.

Locking the door, knowing Simone wasn't going to be home for another two hours, I walked to the bedroom to see how things were going. See if they'd got to the sex part of the fun yet.

PICK

Opening the bedroom door, I stepped in to find Josie standing across the room with her hands on her hips glaring at me. Fuck, it was cute, and I would have told her if I wasn't worried she'd throw something at me. At least she wasn't crying. I'd feel like a real arsehole if I saw her in tears.

"Baby, it's not what you think," I said calmly.

"Then what is it?" she asked with a tremble in her voice.

"How about you sit down?"

"No." She glared.

"Okay, all right." I sighed and ran a hand over my buzz cut. "Precious, you mean everythin' to Eli and me. Fuck, you know we love you and have for a fuckin' long time." Tears pooled in her eyes. Jesus, I knew I never said the words, but she had to have felt it. Striding forward, I cradled her in my arms. Her forehead went to my chest. "I love you, Josie, and there is no way in hell I'd jeopardise it for anythin'."

"Then why lie?" She sniffled.

The bedroom door opened and we both knew it would

be Eli. Still, we didn't turn. He came up beside us and ran his hand down her back.

"We wanted to protect you," I offered.

She groaned and pulled away, glaring once again. Fucking cute.

With her hands on her hips, she snapped, "Don't you both get it? If it has anything to do with either of you, I want to know. I don't want to be put inside a bubble and go along thinking the worst. *I* want to protect you both as well and I can't do that not knowing what's going on." She wiped at her eyes. "I love you both. You have my heart, my soul, and you've both made me stronger. You both know everything about me. But you both need to let me all the way in and tell me everything about you. Please."

While I got my head together, preparing to tell her everything, so nothing was between us again, Eli said, "Sweetheart, you already know everythin' about me. My parents sucked. So I took up a life with a new family. What I didn't expect to find was an even better family within the brotherhood. You and Caden... hell, you both mean a fuckin' heap to me and I'd do anythin' for you both. We can tell you everythin' about us. But please, baby, you gotta know we can't tell you everythin' that goes on with the club."

"I know that," she uttered with a nod. "And I understand it. I just want to be there for you both when you need me. I want to help ease any troubles you both may have. And I need you to know that I'm not the person I used to be. I can handle things, the good, the bad and the very ugly, if I know it helps you both."

Eli smiled at her and held out his hand. She took it and he led her to the bed. I joined them, sitting down on the other side of our woman.

"We're gettin' the picture, sweetheart. We've witnessed you growin' into a beautiful, young, *brave* woman," Eli said.

"Good." She nodded to the floor and then raised her eyes and looked at me. "Can you tell me what's going on, if it doesn't have anything to do with the club?"

"Yeah, precious. I can tell you, but fuck, baby, it ain't good."

She reached her hand up and ran it down my cheek, then took my hand in hers. "I know."

Closing my eyes, I braced myself. Christ, I didn't want to tell her. I wanted to protect her from the fucking wrong things in life, but she was right. We couldn't keep her in a bubble. To know us, she had to know everything that was going on.

"You know I had a shit past. My mum sold my body and got me to do shit I didn't like so she could stay high. What you don't know… the men who, fuck, who took advantage of me." Shit, what would she think of me? I needed to get it out quick, see where I then stood with Josie. Looking to our joined hands, I continued, "I hunted them down and killed them all. But there was one I couldn't find, until recently." I didn't pause for breath, needing to get the words out there. "He's Cameron's father. Eli and I went to meet them. Told his dad that he had to keep his son away from you, or else his past would be shown to the press."

Eli pressed on for me. "We thought he'd listened. It'd been two weeks. Until this mornin'. Caden had a delivery at the compound, which was why we had to go. There was a box. Let's just say Nigel, Cameron's fucked-up father, has told Caden if he doesn't hand you over to his son, he is gonna kill Caden's mum."

She gasped and squeezed my hand. I looked to her and she said, "I'll go. We can't let—"

"No way in hell, Josie," I growled. "I'd go there myself and kill the lotta them before I let them take you. I have enough blood on my hands, what's more—"

"And they deserve it," Josie said quietly.

Eli's eyes widened and my head jerked back. I then uttered, "What?"

She stood suddenly dropping our hands to face us, her hands went to her hips and her eyes glared with an intense gleam to them. She leaned forward to speak her next words and fuck me, she was furious on my behalf. Even her cute nose was scrunched up. "They deserve death, Caden. I know I'm a bad person saying that, but... but... *fuck it*. Your mum's a bitch and if I had a gun myself, I would shoot her for what she put you through. I'm sorry, but I would. People like that, like Nigel," she snarled, "they deserve nothing but death. Hell, if I had my chance I would have loved to have killed David with my bare hands for what he did to me. But I can't." She took a deep breath. Her gaze flittered to the floor and then back up to me. "I'm sorry your mum's in that situation, but she's... crazy, Caden. Crazy to have damaged her son, her own flesh and blood like she did. I know you won't give me up... but, I know you have a big heart, Caden." Christ, she got to her knees in front of me and moved her way between my legs, taking my hands in hers. "I know you don't want your mum's death on your shoulders."

"Fuckin' pure beauty," Eli growled.

Only Josie and Eli could get me to smile on such a fucked-up day. I smiled down at Josie and told her, "You're right, on all accounts, baby. Which is why I called Lan. He's headin' over to Nigel's estate now to see what he can do."

She licked her lips. "Why... why didn't you want to go? He doesn't deserve jail and you could have saved your mum."

Cupping her cheeks in my hands, I said, "I never want to see that woman again. She *is* no one to me, not when I'm finally fuckin' livin'." I kissed her lips and ran my hands to her shoulders before I shrugged. "Besides, if there isn't anythin' Lan can do, at least I tried."

"You're an amazing man, Caden Parker."

"And you're a lioness hidin' under sheep's clothes. I've never heard you swear so much." I chuckled when she glared.

"The moment was right for it." She sighed. "But what about that man who—"

"Even if Lan can find somethin' and he does go to jail, he'll know what hell is. We have brothers on the inside. Just one call and Nigel will want to die, but they won't let him."

Our precious girl nodded and then said, "Good. I'm glad."

"Baby," I groaned. "I just told you I have blood on my hands. I've taken lives and I'm gonna make a call, if it comes to it, to take another life and all you can say is good?"

She bit her bottom lip and her brows drew down like she was confused. "Well, yes. I mean, it's not like you went on a killing spree and killed *innocent* people. They deserved everything they got, and so will Nigel."

That was when Eli and I threw our heads back and laughed.

"How am I being funny?" She glowered and stood.

I sobered and took her hand dragging her to stand between my legs. Her breath caught as she looked down at me. "Can't fuckin' believe how lucky we are, that we have a woman who's everythin' and more. You were made for us, precious. Just us. No one else."

She smiled down at me and before touching her lips to mine, she said, "Never anyone else but you and Eli, always."

"Our girl's comin' into her biker-babe stage," Eli said.

Josie giggled and then gave us a mock glare. "So look out, you don't want to annoy me." She leaned over and kissed Eli, only to pull back and ask, "Is this where we have good make-up sex?"

Eli snorted. I laughed.

"Nothin' good about it, baby," Eli said. "It'll be mind-fuckin'-blowin'."

It was then we heard the front door slam and footsteps coming down the hall.

"Everyone decent in there?" Simone called before knocking on the door.

"No," Eli yelled.

"Never," I said.

"Good," Simone said as she opened the door.

"What happens if I was naked?" Josie asked with a gasp.

"I would enjoy the show." Simone smiled, but her smile faded from her face when she took us all in. "You're not ready?"

"Oh, um, I forgot."

Simone stamped her foot. "Stop distracting her."

"What's this about?" Eli barked.

"Girls' night," Simone sang. "Now that her shit has calmed down, we're heading to the pub."

Standing, I pulled Josie in front of me to hide my hardness for my woman. Wrapping my arms around her shoulders, I said, "Girls' night just turned into girls' and guys' night."

Simone gasped. "You can't."

"Why the fuck not?" Eli demanded.

Simone glared. "We'll be talking about your cocks and how good you are in bed."

Eli shrugged. "Like we give a fuck. What pub? I'll ring the brothers. They can meet us there."

"You're not coming," Simone snapped.

"Try and stop us, woman. Josie's not goin' out without us and that's fuckin' final," I barked.

Simone looked to Josie with pleading eyes. So fucking glad our woman knew the shit wasn't totally over because then she knew we'd want to be by her side. Hell, we'd want it anyway. No fucker was going near our woman.

"Sorry," Josie offered her friend.

"Bloody hell, you're lucky they're good looking," she said and stomped off, but not before she yelled back, "Be ready in half an hour and the pub is called Blow Hard."

CHAPTER SIXTEEN

JOSIE

A night out with my men. I was excited. Yes, we had been on dates, but we had never been to a pub before where there would be dancing and drinking. Plus, Simone had always gone on about how good drunken sex was. My excitement about *that* was an understatement.

When we arrived at Blow Hard, I expected it to be a large, loud and busy place being a pub in Melbourne. However, it wasn't. It was a small pub on a corner. The music wasn't loud where you had to shout over people, and the crowd wasn't over the top. I liked it.

Simone walked ahead dressed in vinyl pants and a red halter top. Eli was next. He and Caden were dressed in their usual; jeans, tees, biker boots and their club vests over the top of their tight tees. Honestly, they looked delicious. I walked down the small hallway where the coat stand was, between Eli and Caden. Simone had talked me into wearing a short denim skirt and a green corset.

Earlier, when I'd walked into the living room, where my men were waiting for us, I thought it funny how their eyes nearly popped out of their heads. Only, they quickly controlled it and Caden growled, "You stick by our side tonight."

"Why?" I asked. I had been looking forward to dancing because it had been so long since I last went out.

"Baby." Eli chuckled. "The way you look, it won't be only *our* dicks bein' hard tonight from watchin' you. Every fuckin' guy will be. They need to know you're claimed by us."

Simone, who was walking down the hall, had heard Eli and burst out laughing. "Maybe tonight will be fun with these two coming along."

"Should I change?" I asked Caden and Eli.

"Fuck no." Caden smiled. "Let's get outta here so we can get back and have our own fun."

"Shit yeah," Eli said, slapping Caden on the shoulder.

From then on, I couldn't wipe the smile from my face. Simone headed straight to the bar across from the front hall. Goodness, the place looked like something out of a western movie. Wooden floor, walls and a bar surrounded us.

I was too busy looking around, I didn't notice Eli had stopped until I walked into him. He moved aside and I smiled at the men in front of me as Caden came up behind me and placed his hands on my shoulders.

"Hi, guys," I said to Dallas, Dodge and Dive. Then I giggled when I realised all their names started with D. "Dive, when did you get here?" I asked, covering my laugh.

"Just yesterday, love. Good to see your smilin' face. Hope these two idiots are treatin' you well."

I couldn't stop the blush, which they all saw and laughed. "I can see they are," Dive teased.

"Holy hotness, Batgirl. Who do we have here?" Simone asked as she sidled up to me and handed me a fruity looking drink.

Even though Dodge and Dallas had been to the apartment before, each time they had, they'd either missed Simone or she was still out with her, now ex, boyfriend.

"Simone, I would like you to meet Dallas, Dodge and Dive. Guys, this is my friend Simone," I offered as I pointed out each one. They were all similarly dressed like Eli and Caden. Jeans, some dark or light tees with their Hawks cut over the top and biker boots. They all looked very handsome, which probably explained why Simone was currently drooling.

Dallas sent her a chin lift. Dodge smiled with a nod and Dive stretched out his hand and took Simone's. "I think I've found my happily ever after." Dive smirked and winked.

Simone laughed. "You play your cards right for the night, I could just be. However, for now, Josie and I are going to that booth over there to talk." She pointed to a booth close by. "Will that be okay, close enough you can both keep an eye on your prize?" Simone smirked at Caden and Eli.

"Smartarse," Eli said.

"Fine." Caden smiled and sent me a wink.

"I wouldn't want her fuckin' far either," Dodge said as Simone steered me to the booth. "She looks fuckin' fine," he added. I heard a slap and looked over my shoulder to see Eli glowering at Dodge who rubbed the back of his head.

While I sat on one side of the booth, giggling at their antics, Simone sat on the other and sighed. "What's wrong?" I asked.

"It feels like it's been so long since we've caught up."

Nodding, I had to agree. Usually, it was just Simone and I; however, with my men in my life, I was occupied. "You've also been busy. But I know what you mean. Please tell me what's been going on with you."

She smiled brightly, her teeth showed and all. "Nothing as exciting as you. Even though I hardly see you,"—she reached across the table and took my hand—"I'm so happy for you, honey. So happy. Never have I see you shine so brightly before. Which is why I'll put up with their bossiness because it's obvious they make you happy and you know you do the same for them, right?"

"Yes. They tell me."

"Good. I'm so glad you have that in life now. But honestly, sweetie, you've got to tell me who is better in bed and who has the biggest dick?"

My head fell back, my eyes to the ceiling and I laughed loudly. So loud I knew I would draw attention and when I looked to my men, they were already watching me, both smiling satisfied grins.

"I'm serious, woman. You have to tell your sister from another mister. I need deets, stat."

A blush rose. "Um, they are both very, very good in bed. And I haven't actually measured their parts."

"What? Get on that woman and let me know." She sat back in her seat and studied me while she drank from her drink. Looking down at mine, I noticed it was already empty. No wonder though, it tasted like heaven. "Have you been with them while the other is in the room?"

Goodness. If Simone was going to grill me about my sex life, I was going to need another drink. Someone must have read my mind because a waiter stood beside our table and placed two more fruity drinks on it.

"Thank you, but who are they from?" I would never take a drink from someone I didn't know.

"The one with the buzz cut," he said with a smile and thumbed behind him to Caden. I waved and mouthed 'thank you' to my man. He winked.

"Aw, isn't that cute. I need me a good man." She pouted and finished her first drink to start on the next as the waiter disappeared.

"We haven't had the chance to talk about Jack, I thought you liked him. What went wrong there?" I asked while swishing my drink around with the straw. I just realised I'd never mentioned to my men I hadn't drank before. I guessed they'd soon find out.

Simone looked away, over to the men and back. Her smile disappeared, only to come back full force, but wrong. It wasn't her usually happy, carefree smile. "Hey now, you didn't answer my question from before. Do they share well?"

"Simone—"

"We're here to have a good night," she snapped.

Drink forgotten, I leaned forward and met her glare with my own. "I know that, honey. And to answer *your* question, yes, they share well, and yes we do it with everyone in the room. Now I want to know what just happened. What aren't you telling me, Simone Michaels?"

She scoffed and turned back to looking at the men. "Wow, they really have brought you out of your shell."

"They have and if you don't talk to me, honey, you won't like what I do next."

Her head snapped back to me. "What?"

"I'll involve them." I gestured with my head to the guys.

"Holy shit." She smiled in a proud way. "You can be manipulative."

"Some say I take after my sister Zara when I want to. She did the same thing to her best friend. Don't make me worry like her friend did to her. Please tell me what's going on. I want to help. You've always been there for me. This time I'm here for you."

She shrugged. "It's nothing really. Jack turned out to be an arse."

I glanced over to see my men watching. They knew something was going on. I could tell by their tense forms.

They were worried. Eli raised his brows at me, but I shook my head.

"Did he do something to you?"

"Nothing I couldn't handle." She smirked, only it was sour.

"Simmy, what happened?"

She rolled he eyes. "He was an arse, that's all."

Frustrating woman. "How was he an arse?"

"I was told, from a trustworthy source, he had a girlfriend. I was just the side piece, because apparently, I'm easy."

My eyes widened. "He had a girlfriend *and* he called you easy?"

She nodded. "Yeah, apparently I'm only good to be someone's side piece. And the easy part came from his friends saying I'd slept with them, when I hadn't. It was just a few kisses. Anyway, it's over."

"Do you need me to get Caden and Eli to rough him up a bit?" I smiled.

Finally, she laughed free and easy. "Thanks, but no. Well, not just yet anyway."

We sat and talked about uni and about Parker being absent for longer than usual. I hadn't had the chance to tell her what Parker had said before he left and when I did, she squealed. "I knew he had a thing for you. The way he looked at you when *you* weren't watching was damn hot."

Shrugging, I said, "I honestly never thought of him in that way. He was nice to look at, but that's it. Though, I do worry about him in a brotherly fashion."

"What do you think his job is?"

We'd pondered that many times and all ideas seemed ridiculous.

"I wouldn't have the foggiest."

"Yeah, me neither. Uh-oh, looks like you've got competition over there. Actually, knowing your guys, it's not competition just annoying trolls."

Looking over to the men standing at the bar, I saw they'd received some visitors. In the type of hussies. Two girls in slutty dresses, one with peroxide blonde hair and the other had long black hair. The blonde was standing beside Caden and the other was next to Eli. I couldn't really say they were hussies. I didn't know them. They could be nice women… if they weren't rubbing their boobs against my men's arms.

Standing, I stalked my way over to them. Dodge and Dive saw me coming and started laughing. Maybe they hadn't seen my scowl before. Dallas stood leaning against the bar with a smirk upon his face.

Ignoring them, I stepped between my men. Before I could say anything, Simone got there first. I hadn't even realised she'd followed. "I wouldn't bother, ladies."

The women looked at her and then me. They both gave us the once over and dismissed us.

Now *that* annoyed me.

"Excuse me," I started. They looked back.

"Go away, we got here first," the blonde snapped.

"No." I glared. "I believe I got there first when I had both of them last night in my bed." Manly chuckles surrounded us. Including my two men who I was shooting my own glares at. "Now, please get your hands off them." Alcohol encouraged my snarky behaviour and the need for all to know Caden and Eli were mine.

"You're kidding me, right? *You* had both of these guys?"

I harrumphed when blondie turned back to Caden and whispered something in his ear. I had to admit I liked that he tried to lean away from her, but she wasn't having it. Her hand went to the side of his face.

Taking her wrist in my hand, I brought it down. She shook me off and then her friend stepped, with a sway, up into my face. "Touch her again and we have got problems, bitch." Her breath stunk of cigarettes and bourbon.

"I'm sorry, but I'm not looking for trouble tonight. I would just like it if you would both leave those two"—I pointed to Caden and Eli—"alone."

"Go, Josie," Dodge bellowed.

I sent him a glare.

The black-haired one laughed in my face. "I don't think so, bitch."

"Shut the fuck up," Eli snarled.

"Eli, I'm handling it," I snapped.

"Babe," was all he said with humour.

Which made the one in my face turn to look at him. Being stupid, she let what he'd said go and looked back to me.

"Please, just leave and go find some other men to try and snag for the night. These two are not them. They *are* mine," I said with confidence.

"Claimed," Dive shouted with a laugh.

Simone stepped forward and said, "You both don't get it, being so dumb and drunk doesn't help. You and your stinky pussies aren't wanted or needed here, so fuck off."

"You bitch," the blonde screamed and went to slap Simone.

However, her hand was suddenly stopped by Caden wrapping his hand around her wrist. She turned into him and said in a sickly sweet voice. "Handsome, tell them to get out of here."

Caden looked down at her with disgust and threw her arm back before she could run it up his chest. She stumbled back. He glared down at her and growled, "It's you both who need to fuck off." He looked to me. "Josie." Stepping up to him he shifted me in front of him so I was facing the women and placed his hands on my hips. "See what I have in my hands, she's all class. You ladies need to take a page outta her book and stop openin' your legs to any guy. You give shit to her and her friend again, you'll have to deal with us and trust me, it won't be pleasurable. Now get the fuck outta our sight."

With that, he ignored them. They stood there in shock when Caden started kissing my neck, and then, not to be out done, Eli stepped up to my side. He grinned wickedly down at me and touched his lips to mine. Before I closed my eyes and all sane thoughts left—like they did every time my men paid attention to me—I looked out the corner of my eye to see both women with slack jaws and wide eyes.

Eli bit my bottom lip and I was a goner. I closed my eyes

and enjoyed the moment with my men. Knowing we had an audience no longer registered, nor did I worry. Nothing could get me down when I had my men with me.

Eli was the first to pull back and then Caden, who wrapped his arms around my waist and kissed my forehead.

"Fuckin' hell, does she commit like that all the time, even for just a kiss?" Dive asked.

"Hell yeah." Eli smirked and winked when my cheeks started to heat.

"Christ, I need to find myself some *sweet* pussy," Dallas muttered before he turned back to the bar, banged his fist on it and ordered another round of drinks.

CHAPTER SEVENTEEN

JOSIE

*T*he night was one of the best ones in my life. Simone and I drank, danced and had the most fun. If any guy came up to me on the dance floor, I froze. But all Simone had to do was point over to the bar and once they spotted a scowling Eli and Caden, who would shake their heads, the guy would quickly flee the scene.

By the end of the night, I was slightly intoxicated, the feeling liberating. Never would I have had the guts to walk up to my men, after dancing once again with Simone, lean into the middle of them and state, what I thought was quietly, "I would like to go home and have my wicked way with you both."

"Fuck me," I heard Dallas say.

"Jesus, suddenly I feel like singin', 'Me and my hand tonight'," Dodge barked.

Dive didn't say anything, because his mouth was very busy with Simone's tongue in it. I'd asked her as we danced if she was taking him home for the night. She shook her head and said, "Honey, you know I'm all talk most of the time. Doesn't mean I can't let my mouth have a little fun."

"We're outta here," Eli growled as he looked down at me with lust in his eyes.

It didn't take us long to drive home, but it felt like forever. I was in the back with Simone, who was half asleep, while my men were up in the front. I liked the way Caden would grip the steering wheel tightly, like he was wishing we were already home. And Eli would clench and unclench his jaw time and time again.

They were horny and I bet if I could see their groins, they would be hard.

Suddenly, I really wanted to see their groins.

Or even their chests.

Heck, I would even go for their feet.

Skin, I needed their skin naked, their bodies under me, over me and inside of me.

"Fuckin' hurry up or she'll be comin' in the car with the sounds she's making," Eli growled.

"Lucky bitch," Simone slurred.

As soon as Caden pulled up to the curb, Caden had his door open. He was helping me out and guiding my swaying body into the apartment building, while Eli got Simone out of the car, into his arms and carried her in because she'd passed out.

While I went to the bathroom to freshen up and tried not to fall over, Eli put Simone in her room. When I came out of the bathroom, I noticed her bedroom door was shut. I smiled to myself. I was glad it was shut because I was prepared to make some noise with my men.

Wow, I was a lucky bitch.

Opening my bedroom door, my eyes landed on an already naked Eli who was laying on the bed with his arms behind his head. Caden was standing at the end of the bed and before I'd come in, he'd been admiring Eli's naked body. Who wouldn't? They both sported beautiful, sculpted bodies. Caden smiled at me as he pulled his tee over his head and then shoved down his jeans.

Soon enough, I had two naked forms in my room.

"Babe, you comin' to bed or you just gonna stand there and admire us all night?" Eli teased.

"Um…" It was a hard question. Admiring was nice, but feeling them would be even better. Stepping in the room more, I closed the door behind me. My hands went to my hips and I wiggled out of my skirt. Next, I kicked it off along with my shoes. My hands went behind me to my corset top to reach the zipper; however, I found it hard to find. My body shifted this way and that to try and reach it.

A laughing Caden came over and helped. He turned my back to him and slowly unzipped my corset while trailing his lips over my shoulders.

"Did we tell you how fuckin' hot you looked tonight?"

"N-no." I sighed when the corset was free and falling to the floor.

A light tap on the bottom and Caden growled, "Go see Eli before I bend you over and fuck you right here and now."

Was there something wrong with doing that?

Caden smiled. "Precious," he said with a touch of his lips on mine. "Eli wants to tell you how good you looked."

Nodding, I stepped around him and smiled to Eli on the bed. He grinned back and held out his arm to me. I bounded on to the bed and then lay next to him. He got to his elbow so he could look down at me. "Caden's right, you were fuckin' smokin' tonight. Not like you aren't always, but tonight, I had to restrain myself from kickin' a lot of arse because of all the eyes on you."

"I know how that feels," I said honestly. "I felt like bitch-slapping a few women as well. I don't think we should go out anymore. I'd like to keep you both home and to myself for the rest of my life."

Both of my men laughed.

"Can't have that, baby," Caden said as he kneeled on the end of the bed. "We like showin' off the beauty we have in our lives, and bed."

"Damn." I giggled.

"Sweetheart, you drunk?"

"Just a little." I smiled.

"Fuckin' awesome." Eli winked.

Hands were at my hips and I looked down to see Caden pulling my panties down. I lifted so it was easier as he dragged them down my legs. Eli started kissing me. I wrapped my arms around his neck. He growled low when I pulled all his weight on top of me. I wanted to feel his chest against mine. Our heated skin touched and it felt wonderful.

Eli's lips moved to my jaw, my neck and then he whispered in my ear, "I need to eat your perfect pussy. I have to taste you, lick you."

"Yes," I moaned my reply.

I looked down my body as Eli moved to his knees and Caden spread my legs for him, running his hands up and down from thighs to ankles. He moved back and Eli shifted between my legs. He lay on his stomach and blew a cool breath on my hot pussy causing me to shiver in anticipation.

Even from the first lick, from bottom to top, it had me closing my eyes, my back arching, my hands fisting the sheets and me moaning.

"Roll on your side," I heard Caden order. Opening my eyes, I looked down to see that he wasn't looking at me but Eli.

"What...?" Eli started, but stopped and looked from Caden up to me.

"Roll on your side," Caden growled.

Why would Caden want Eli on his side?

Unless... Goodness.

"Please," I begged. Since that first night I had seen them pleasuring each other, I had wanted to see more from them, but I was afraid to ask in case they weren't all that into it.

Eli adjusted himself to his side, his erection facing Caden. Both Eli and I watched as Caden lay on his stomach, his face just inches away from Eli's hardness.

Getting to my elbows so I could see better, I watched with rapt attention as Caden took hold of Eli's cock, brought his face forward and opened his mouth to slowly glide his lips over Eli's penis.

A throb started in my core.

"Jesus," Eli groaned and laid his hand on Caden's head as it bobbed up and down on Eli's dick.

"That's beautiful," I uttered.

Caden didn't stop his assault, but Eli looked up at me with wide eyes. "You like watchin'?"

"Yes." I nodded.

"Fuck, that felt good. Do it again," he told Caden, looking down at him. "Yeah, fuck," Eli groaned loudly. He gazed back up at me. "Christ, you do like watchin' him suck me," he said, taking in my hooded eyes, my heaving chest and then looking down to my pussy. "Hell, you're drenched," he commented as he ran his fingers up and down, spreading my juices everywhere. As I watched Caden, I also watched Eli as he licked his lips and bent his head to taste me.

"Goodness." I sighed. Eli's movements turned frantic. He licked, sucked and tongued in a fast rhythm; all of it was driving me insane. Too soon I felt the tightness in my lower stomach and then it gushed straight down. "I'm coming!" I yelled and thrust my pussy up onto Eli's face more.

Before I was with it, I was pulled up and straddling Caden's hips. My lowered gaze caught his as he shifted me back a little, his hand went between us and then I was brought forward straight onto his length. I threw my head back and screamed as he slammed hard into me.

"Fuck, yes," he yelled. His arms went around to my back. He brought me closer so our chests touch, my forehead went to his shoulder as I rocked back and forth on his cock. "So you liked watchin', baby?"

"Very much," I said.

"Let's share it then." I pulled back to look at him. He smirked, kissed me passionately and then turned to Eli who was beside us on his knees, his hand fisting his cock. I moaned from the sight. "Stand up," Caden said to Eli who smiled and stood with his feet on the bed. As I rocked on Caden's cock, Eli bent a little and placed his dick between Caden and me. I grinned and slid my lips up and down my side of Eli's cock as Caden did the same on the other.

God, it was beautiful. All of us.

"Hmm," I whimpered against Eli's cock and I felt another orgasm building.

"Christ, that looks good," Eli growled. I glanced up to see him watching Caden and I licking his dick.

Caden's head went back and he groaned out, "Fuck, I'm gonna come in our girl's tight pussy."

"Jesus, not yet," Eli snapped and brought Caden's mouth back to his dick. "Yes, fuck, yes, like that. God, that's it." With his hands on the back of my head and Caden's, he fucked our faces. "Shit, fuck. I'm gonna come," Eli grunted. He withdrew his dick and started fisting it, white streams of cum shot out all over Caden's and my chest.

My rocking on Caden's cock was faster. Caden gripped my hips. I leaned back, my hands on his knees as I thrust up and down on him.

"Baby," Caden groaned. "Fuck, Josie," he growled.

"Oh, Caden, yes," I mumbled as I came, my walls clenched around Caden as I felt him swell inside of me.

"Fuck," he growled on his first shot of cum inside of me. "Jesus, yes," he grunted deeply as I still rode him until all spasms stopped.

My guys were the best ever.

CHAPTER EIGHTEEN

PICK

I woke in Parker's room with a fucking smile on my face and that was because last night had rocked my world. I thought I'd come hard before, but nothing like last night when watching both Josie and Eli just let go and enjoy the moment, enjoy each other with me.

Even though I was asked to stay in the room last night to sleep, I still came in here, why? Because we needed that. We needed to take turns sleeping with Josie on our own. I fucking loved when it was my turn. Waking up with my light beside me was goddamn perfect. Christ, even when I wasn't waking up beside her, I still knew I was only metres away from her and fucking Eli.

Hell, never had I thought I'd... *love* a guy like I did him. It was strange, but totally worth it. When I got to see Eli tease

Josie about something or when he'd get her to laugh, it was a fun sight to watch.

I couldn't wait to get into our own place. We'd even started packing over the last week. It wasn't long before we moved. Nerves were present, and hope, both about how we'd keep it going perfect like it already was. I knew there'd be times when things would seem shit, after an argument or something, but the making-up part would be worth it.

A knock on the front door got me out of bed and stalking my way to it in boxers. Josie had a late night and I wanted her to sleep in before her shift later at the diner.

Opening the door, my jaw clenched when I spotted Lan standing there with a sour look on his face. "Fuck," I growled.

"That about sums it up, man." He lifted his chin. "Can I come in?"

Stepping back, I nodded. "Take a seat, I'll just grab some pants." I stomped off to the room and slipped on some jeans, fuck the tee, I knew what Lan had to say wasn't going to be good, better get it over and done with.

I'd just made it back in the living room when we heard a door down the hall open. Lan and I turned in that direction as a smiling Josie walked out wearing a silk robe that clung to her sexy curves and Eli was following her in a pair of jeans like me.

Josie saw me first, her eyes not moving from my face until she walked up to me, wrapped her arms around my neck and kissed me. She pulled back and said, "Morning."

"Hey, precious."

"So it's all true… the both of you and Josie?"

Josie stiffened in my arms. I was fucking pleased she saw nothing and no one but me when her eyes had landed on me first. And it was cute when her cheeks tinted once finding out we had a guest. I wanted to take her back to the room and fuck her hard, but that'd have to be waylaid until Lan had finished shitting in our hands with the bad news he had to deliver.

"Lan, I-I didn't see you there."

He smirked. "Obviously."

"Shit," Eli barked.

"What's going on?" Josie asked.

"Baby, you wanna go get dressed and we'll—"

"No." She glared. Her hands went to her hips. I saw Lan turn to hide his smile. "If it has anything to do with that… pompous arse, then I want to know."

"Right," I said and then smiled, bringing her in close. Even though she tried to fight it, I kissed her pissed attitude away. Pulling back, I said, "Sit down then."

Her eyes went wide for a second and then she uttered, "Well, okay then."

"Lucky bastards," Lan muttered as he sat in the chair leaving the couch for me, Eli, and Josie in the middle.

"Don't we know it." Eli grinned and curled his arm around Josie, who was once again blushing.

"Um… Lan, how are you liking Melbourne?" Josie asked.

"Yeah, been all right. Way bigger than Ballarat."

"You talked to Memphis yet?" I asked.

"Yeah, man. In tight, better when you two come aboard

soon. We'll need the help. Got some"—he glanced at Josie and then back to me—"people in the department I don't trust."

"We'll be in soon, hopefully, depends on what you have to tell us," I said.

"We right to talk?" he gestured to Josie with his chin. I nodded. "Okay then, we went to Mr Peterson's house yesterday afternoon. Of course, we didn't have a warrant so all we could do was ask him some questions." He ran a hand over his face. "At the time, I wasn't sure your mum was even there, Pick. But… shit. We had to leave, man, and it wasn't until late last night a neighbour called and complained about shoutin'. They thought they heard a gunshot. I drove over there with some blues. The front door was open." He paused.

"Just spit it out, brother," I growled.

He nodded. "We went in. Found Mr Peterson in his library, gunshot wound to the head. He's dead." I felt Josie stiffen beside me. "We searched the house. Found your mum downstairs in the basement… She's dead also, man."

Fuck.

I waited for the sting of her death to hit me, only it didn't come.

"What about Cameron?" Eli asked.

"The son?" Lan questioned.

"Yeah." Eli nodded.

"You guys got a beef with him as well?"

"You could say that. He hassled Josie for a while. Wanted her for himself, wasn't gonna happen," Eli explained. "You could say he even tried to have his dad get her for him."

"That explains his… " he started saying to himself, looking at the floor, and then he looked to me and asked, "Your mum?" Lan asked.

"Yeah," I spat.

"Sorry about your loss, brother," Lan offered.

I snorted and just about jumped when I felt Josie's hand touch my back. "No loss really. She was never a good mother."

"Right, well, there's somethin' else you guys need to know."

Shit. Lan actually bit his bottom lip, as if he wished he didn't have to say what was coming next.

"What?" Eli growled.

"Ah." His gaze roamed over Josie for a second. "We searched the rest of the house. Sorry, Josie, but that Cameron kid, he's kinda into you."

"We know this," I barked.

Lan shook his head. "No, brother. I mean he's really into your woman. So much so his bedroom walls are lined with pictures of her."

Josie gasped. Her hand flew over her mouth.

The detective ran a hand across the back of his neck. "Did you guys go to the drive-in recently?"

Our first date. The little fucker was there photographing us.

"And Eli, you and Josie went to a carnival."

"Motherfucker," Eli spat.

"You need to know we're searchin' for Cameron. Not only for his obsession with Josie, but we believe it was him who shot his dad and your mum. Cameron's mum is outta town on some trip at the moment."

Motherfucking Cameron.

The little cocksucker took away my chance for retribution, and took away the chance to show my mum I was finally fucking clean and had beauty on my arm. *And* he wanted our woman in a sick-as-fuck way.

"We'll let you know if we spot him." I smiled. Lan searched my face, looked to the floor, and shook his head, but I was sure we all saw the smile he was fighting.

Lan was a good guy. Even though he was a detective, he still had our backs. I knew if I pushed the matter, he wouldn't bother looking for Cameron. Hell, either way, if Lan found him or we did, both ways Cameron would wish his life had ended with his dad's.

"I really gotta find another job." Lan sighed.

"No need, brother, you stay clean always," I said.

"You do good in the system and from what you said, you'll need our help soon enough." Eli grinned.

"Yeah, I reckon so. What's the plan then?"

"Stay vigilant. He'd still want Josie. He's too fuckin' fascinated by her in all the wrong ways. So we'll keep her safe."

"I'll look on my end, but if you, any of you, need anythin'... "

"Really 'preciate it, man."

As soon as the door closed behind Lan, Josie was straddling my hips. "Are you okay?" she asked with concern in her eyes.

My hand went to her neck. "Yeah, baby, I'm good."

She cocked her head to the side. Cute. "You sure?"

I smiled. "'Course, but maybe you should worry about your freedom. You know you won't be gettin' any alone time. Not until that dick's outta the way."

"I'm okay with that, as long as I have both of you by my side."

"Always be at your side, woman."

She grinned. "Good. Now, are you sure you're okay? I mean, sucks you don't get to take that... schmuck out for what he did to you, but... your mum."

"Precious, I promise you I'm good. Unless you wanna make me feel even better?" I raised my brows at her and smirked.

She giggled. "I could do that."

And she did.

CHAPTER NINETEEN

JOSIE

*C*aden moving in bed registered before the sound of ringing from his phone. "Hello," he answered, his voice sleepy. In the next second, he sat up. "Yeah, we're on our way." He threw the sheet from his body and got out of bed.

"Caden?" I questioned, sitting up. My hands gripped the sheets because from the way his body tensed, I knew something was wrong.

"Eli," Caden yelled, then turned to me after donning a tee and jeans. "Get up, precious, we gotta get goin'."

I rose to my knees on the bed. "What's going on, Caden?"

"Please, baby. Please just get up and get dressed." His tone was gentle, but his jaw was clenched tightly.

God, no. It was something bad.

"Eli," Caden yelled again.

The bedroom door banged open and Eli stumbled in from sleeping in Parker's room wearing only boxers. "What's all the yellin' 'bout?"

"Get dressed, wake Simone and get her ready. She's comin' with us. We gotta get back to Ballarat, *now*." Caden faced me. "Precious, move. Get dressed, somethin' warm. We're ridin' out in five."

"Pick?" Eli queried.

Caden shook his head and barked, "Now!" Eli disappeared from the doorway. I heard him open Simone's door with a bang, next her scream of surprise and then Eli ordering her up and dressed.

"Josie. Get up, woman."

"It's something bad, isn't it?"

"Baby, come on. I need you focused for the ride. Please just trust me." He reached out his hand toward me. I looked from his face to it. He needed me to stay focused for the ride. He didn't want me a mess on the bike in case it caused an accident. Which meant it was heartbreaking news.

Oh, God. Who's hurt?

Be strong.

Get there and stay strong.

For now.

"Right," I uttered and placed my hand in Caden's. He pulled me from the bed and helped me get dressed in jeans, a tee, then a thermal long-sleeved top as well as a hooded jumper. Looking to the clock it said two in the morning, no wonder he was dressing me warm. But if I didn't get outside soon, I would pass out with the amount of clothing I had on.

We walked from the bedroom, with Caden behind me leading me with his hand on my lower back, down the hall to the living room where Simone was already waiting with a panicked look on her face. Her hands restlessly played with her hair and she gnawed on her bottom lip.

"Josie?" she asked.

Shaking my head, I said, "I don't know, honey. Something's happened in our hometown." I felt Caden's heat from his hand on my back disappear. He walked back down the hall to, no doubt Parker's room, where Eli was, to fill him in on what was going on.

Stepping up closer to Simone, I whispered, "Whatever it is, it's bad, Simmy."

Before my eyes, Simone took a deep breath. Her hands went to my shoulders and her eyes hardened. She was preparing herself for whatever it was because she knew she'd have to be there for me. It was why Caden chose to wake her to come with us, and also the fact that Cameron was still out there somewhere. "Whatever it is, we'll deal, yeah?"

"Let's move," Eli ordered as he strolled into the living room dressed in jeans, his biker boots and a leather jacket zipped all the way up. He didn't need to turn for me to know the back of his jacket held the logo to the Hawks MC.

"Where's Caden?" I asked.

"He's coming, sweetheart. Just had to make a call." As he

passed Simone and myself, he bent and lightly touched his lips to mine. "We'll meet him outside."

"Okay," I mumbled and started for the door after him.

Simone got close and whispered, "Have I told you lately that you're so goddamn lucky?" I tried for a smile over my shoulder, but it deflated. Simone took my hand in hers and squeezed it as we descended the stairs.

Outside, Eli helped, first Simone, with her helmet and then me. Just as we were getting our gloves on as well, Caden appeared wearing similar clothes to Eli. Without a word, he straddled his bike, placed on his helmet and gestured with his head for me to climb on the back.

"Looks like I get to have my arms around you, handsome," Simone said to Eli.

I couldn't help myself from saying, "Just this once."

Eli chuckled, ran his hand down my arm and went to his bike. I watched him climb on and then Simone slipped on behind him before I got on Caden's bike. As soon as my arms were wrapped around him, Caden kicked his Harley to life and we roared off into the early hours of the morning.

The ride, what would usually take an hour and a half only took us an hour. I was grateful there were no police on the roads with the speed Caden and Eli had been doing. I presumed we would be heading to a family member's house, or even the compound. However, when we pulled up out the front of the local hospital, my heart dipped to my stomach.

Simone and Eli were already at our side before I even

unstuck myself and found enough courage to slip off the bike. Eli came right up to me and helped me remove the helmet and gloves. I stood still and stared up at the entrance of the hospital.

"Why here?" Simone uttered the question that was on my mind.

Before anyone answered, my eyes brimmed with tears when I spotted a familiar face striding toward us. "No," was whispered past my dry lips.

Zara, my sister with her baby bump belly, came out the front doors and then ran to us. Her eyes red, her face blotchy from crying hard. "Josie," she sniffed before flinging herself at me. Her arms circled my waist, but shock weighed down my reaction to embrace her back. Instead, I stared over her shoulder to see her husband Talon walking our way.

Zara pulled back, her hands going to my face. My eyes sought out her face as her eyes filled with tears.

"No," I uttered.

She bit her bottom lip and nodded. "It's Dad. H-he… " She took a deep breath just as Talon stopped behind his wife. He leaned around her to kiss my cheek briefly and then stood tall, his arms winding around Zara's middle.

"I-I, *what?*" was all I could manage.

Zara, unable to speak as she started sobbing, wrapped me into her arms again. Talon's hands went to her sides, at her waist. He met my watery gaze and said, "Richard had a heart attack, Josie. They're not sure he'll live through the night."

Richard.

Dad.

Heart attack.

Dying.

No!

No, no, no. Not him. Not Dad, not the man who took me in, who showed me I was worth loving. No, please.

My lips went between my teeth to try and stop the onslaught of emotions. I bit down on them, finally wrapping my arms around my sister.

He has to live. He has to. The man, my dad was too good to die.

"Josie," was called from behind Talon.

Lifting my head from Zara's shoulder and wiping my eyes, I saw Mattie, my brother, standing just outside the doorway, looking defeated.

"Honey, he wants to see you."

No. I couldn't. It was too much. I couldn't see him. *Oh, God. It will wreck me. I'll be lost once again.*

Not my dad. Please.

"Come on," Zara whispered. "You can do this."

But I couldn't.

My head shook back and forth. No words came to me though.

Zara either stepped away or was shifted from in front of me. Caden and Eli filled her spot instead. Each took a hand of mine.

"Precious," Caden said sadly. "You need to see him. You need to say goodbye."

My eyes shut tight, my head bowed, and I shook it again and again.

"I-I can't," I sobbed.

"Sweetheart, he needs you." I felt Eli kiss my head. "Be our strong girl just for a little longer. For your dad, baby. He wants to see his girl."

In the background, I heard Zara wailing, no doubt, into Talon's chest.

Dad wants me in there.

Oh, God.

He's dying.

"Josie," Mattie called with a pleading tone.

My balled fists went to my eyes. I rubbed them hard. My body wouldn't stop shivering, my eyes wouldn't stop crying and my stomach wouldn't settle. Still, I had to ignore all of it for my dad. I had to walk in there… somewhat composed.

Straightening my shoulders, I removed my hands and reached out to my men. They both took a hand each and together, we walked into the hospital, only to pause when I hugged my brother tightly.

We'd made it to the fourth floor and out of the elevator before my composure slipped when I saw my mum striding our way. My hands were dropped just as Mum wrapped her arms around me, one hand to my waist the other to the back of my head, where she pulled it forward into her shoulder.

"I-is he in pain?" I asked.

"No, darling. They're taking good care of him." She pulled back and wiped my fresh tears away. She bit her bottom lip. Tears filled her own eyes and I knew what she was about to say was going to wreck me. "I-I think he's holding out to see you, sweetie."

I sucked my lip in and bit down. My head falling back, my watery eyes to the ceiling.

Yes. That wrecked me.

Because it meant he wasn't going to be with us for much longer.

Oh, God. Please, please no, please don't take him.

"Mum," Mattie said. "Come sit down while Josie's in there."

Glancing down, I gave her a quick kiss on the cheek as Mattie whispered the room number in my ear. I took hold of my men's hands again and they walked with me down the hall. We stopped outside the room and already I could hear the machines beeping away, keeping my dad alive.

"Go in, precious. We'll be right here."

Nodding, I squeezed both their hands and turned the corner into the room. A need to run back out was strong when I saw my strong, sweet, funny dad laying in the hospital bed looking pale, withdrawn and tired.

His head turned slowly and, oh God, he smiled a big smile at me like I had just hung the moon for him.

My bottom lip trembled, but I bit it. I wiped furiously at my eyes.

"Baby girl," he uttered, his hand shifted on the bed and stretched out to me.

I ran to him, to his side, my hand circling his where I

gently pulled it up to my cheek. "Dad," I whispered, tears streaming down my face.

"Oh, baby girl, no crying. God must need me up there."

Shaking my head, I said, "But I need you here."

He smiled sadly at me and my heart cracked. "No, baby girl. You no longer need me. You've grown into... " he took a deep shuddering breath that shattered me. "G-grown into a beautiful strong woman and you have not one, but two men willing to take on the world for you."

"I still need my dad." I sobbed, my head resting gently onto his shoulder. His hand slid to the back of my head.

"You have always deserved much love in your life, baby girl, and I was glad I got to be one of those people to love you."

Oh, God, my sweet dad.

It wasn't fair. None of it was fair.

"Now, I... " Looking up to him, I saw he was struggling with not only words but keeping his eyes open. He cleared his throat. "I need you to know, having you come into our lives, baby girl, it made it that much richer. I love you and I don't want you to be sad. I want you to live your life to the fullest and you tell those boys of yours, if they don't take care of my girl, I will come back and haunt their arses."

A burst of laughter left my lips.

Sobering, I said, "I love you, Dad. You know I appreciate everything you've done. You and Mum taught me the world wasn't dark. You showed me I could be loved and cared for." I broke off on a sob when I saw tears in his eyes. They fell like mine. "Dad... "

"My sweet, baby girl, grown so much." He took a deep breath. "Your mum will need some help after... " *Oh, God.* He clenched his jaw as his lips trembled. "After I pass."

Nodding, I whispered, "I'll help her."

"I know, Josie. I know. I've been a lucky man having such great kids. A very lucky man." He reached for my hand and brought it to his lips to kiss it. "Baby girl, when... when I go, I'll go in peace."

Shaking my head, I cried, "Dad—"

"No, Josie. I want you to know, I'll be going in peace because I have lived a life full of happiness and love. You helped make that happen."

Taking in an unstable breath, I nodded again and again.

"Love you, kiddo. So much."

My other hand went over my mouth to hide my choking sob. Once under control, I leaned down, kissed Dad's forehead and told him, "I love you so much, Dad."

The door opened behind me. I looked over my shoulder to see Mum, Zara, Talon, Mattie and Julian enter. Not only them, but my gorgeous men with concern for me in their eyes, silently walked in.

Two hours after I arrived, my dad drifted off to sleep... never waking again.

CHAPTER TWENTY

JOSIE

The next two days were painful. After leaving the hospital a wreck, I went back to my parents' house with Zara, Talon, Mattie, Julian, Simone and my men. The day was a blur. We all sat at the table drinking coffee, all silent in our own thoughts. Simone was in a spare room in the house, getting some sleep. I think she also left so it was just the family. I looked over to Julian to see him rubbing Zara's belly.

I'd missed out on so much in the last two years.

I'd missed my brother proposing to his partner and then the announcement of Zara and Talon willing to give the precious gift of life to Mattie and Julian.

Two years had been too long.

What hurt the most, out of everything, I'd missed the chance to spend more time with my dad.

If I would have known... no, even then, with notice, I couldn't have prepared myself for his loss.

Regret. So much regret for not coming home.

Of being selfish.

"Josie?" Mum said.

I looked up to her and whispered, "I'm sorry. I... I should have been here. I should have visited and now... " My eyes teared. Caden placed his arm around my shoulders and Eli grabbed my hand. "Now, I'll never get to spend time with him again."

"Sweetie," Mum started. She reached over the table with her own tears showing and held her hand out for my free one. I took it and she said, "Don't be sorry. We knew you had to find yourself. We both cherish the time we had with you under our roof, but Josie girl, you needed your time away. If we hadn't known it, we wouldn't have let you leave. Even though you had some trouble... I'm still glad you went, because you wouldn't have opened your heart for the two men beside you. And they wouldn't have pulled their thumbs out of their arses about you either." Laugher sounded. Mum shook my hand. "It all worked out." She smiled. "Richard... " She closed her eyes and bit down on her bottom lip. Upon opening them, she said, "H-he would have already told you, but he's so very proud of you, Josie. Just like I am."

She stood from the table and went to the sink to place her mug in, but she stood there staring out the back window above the counter. "Talon, you had better go rescue Deanna from your tribe. We need the babies here to tell them, to let them know... "

"Mum," Zara uttered. "They'll be fine there for a while. Clary and Blue are there helping her and Griz. You need to get some sleep."

Mattie got up from his seat and walked over to Mum. He placed his arm around her shoulders. Only she shrugged him off and turned to the room at large. "No, life must go on. I need my grandbabies. They need to know... they have to learn... he's gone." Her face crumbled, her body sagging. Mattie supported her. Though, seeing him struggle, Eli went around the table to take her other side. With her eyes to the floor, she whispered, "It feels like a part of me has died with him." She leaned into her son more. "H-how am I supposed to go on without him?"

Mattie closed his eyes. Tears fell to his cheeks and he shook his head. "I don't know, Mum. What I do know is that Dad would want us to."

Mum nodded. "He would. But right now I don't want to," she cried. "I can't do this. I can't go on without him. He was my everything." Her hands went to her face and she sobbed into them.

It broke my heart even more.

Talon stood abruptly. He went to Mum and picked her up in his arms. "Kitten," he growled. "Josie, Matthew," he added and then he strode out of the room and down the hall with us following. He deposited Mum in her room on her bed, turned and went to his wife. He cupped her cheeks, wiping away her tears. "Be with her, cry with her, talk to her. About good times and bad. You all need sleep. Eventually that will come. You take care of her and then, after, I'll take care of you. Just like their men will for them." He gestured to Mattie and me. With that, he kissed her soundly on the lips and left the room, closing the door behind him.

So that was what we did. I cuddled into Mum's back. Zara was at her front and Mattie lay just behind Zara with his arm over her waist, holding Mum's hand. We talked and listened to one another. We cried... a lot, and then, eventually we did sleep.

THE NEXT DAY Talon brought my nieces and nephews home. Simone was out food shopping with Julian. They didn't want to overwhelm the kids with too many people in the house. The toddlers, Drake and Ruby, wouldn't really understand the situation. But Maya who was now nine and Cody at fifteen knew something was wrong as soon as they walked in. The little ones ran straight for their mum and grandma, who were sitting on the couch with Mattie. Maya, and then Cody, both stopped still at the front door. It took Talon's hand on each of their backs to force them forward so he could close the door.

Maya studied her mum and then grandma. Cody studied everyone and then asked, "Where's Grandpa?"

Zara's bottom lip trembled. Cody took that in, his head bowed, his eyes to his feet and he uttered, "Shit."

Maya, watching her mother's lips tremble asked, "Mum, where's Grandpa?" Zara, unable to voice her thoughts because her emotions were taking over, said nothing. "Mum," Maya yelled. "Grandpa?" she called.

I stepped away from Eli and Caden and got to my knees. Taking after her mum, Maya was not tall in size. On my knees, we came face to face. "Aunty Jose," she whispered, fright plain to see in her eyes. Oh, God, she knew, she knew what was happening, but she didn't want it to be real.

My hand cupped her cheek and I told her, "He's gone, Maya. G-grandpa passed away from a heart attack."

She shook her head back and forth saying, "No, no, no, no," over and over again.

"Grandpa back?" Drake asked from on Zara's knee.

She looked down to her three-year-old son and shook her head. "No, baby, Grandpa won't be back."

"Mum," Maya cried. "Mum," she sobbed and next she was in her dad's arms, her face buried in his stomach and she held on for dear life as she wailed. I stood and went back to my men. I rested my head against Caden's chest and held Eli's hand.

"Cody, here boy," Talon ordered.

Looking over to Cody, he stood off to the side, his head still down and he shook his head.

"Cody," Talon's tone was soft.

Cody looked up and glared at his dad. "Why him? Why someone who's so good? Why not some fuckin' arse who does bad shit?" He turned and punched the wall, his fist going through the plaster. He was his father's son.

"Cody," Talon growled.

"Leave him, Talon," Mum said. She placed Ruby, who was taking it all in, in Mattie's arms and got up. She walked to Cody. Her hand went to his back while he leaned his forehead against the wall.

"Cody," she whispered.

"No," he uttered.

"It's okay," she choked.

"It's not, Grandma. It's not gonna be okay. It's not fair."

"You're right, my child, it's not and we can get pissed all we want about it. We can scream, yell and swear because none of it is fair. Your grandpa should not be gone from this world, but he is and what's not fair about that is there's nothing we can do about it." She sighed. "But, Cody, what you need to learn is, you've got to let the pain out. You can't bottle it up and take it out on everyone or items in my household. You've got to let it go, Cody."

He spun to face her, his face red. "No, I can't. If I do, it will be real," he yelled, tears in his eyes. "It can't be real. It can't be."

"Oh, baby," Mum uttered, a sob caught in her throat. "But it is real."

"Fuck," he yelled. "Goddammit," he screamed and then... oh, God, then he fell forward onto Mum's shoulder and cried.

That was when I let myself go once again. It was too hard seeing the pain through such a young person's eyes.

THE DAY of our dad's funeral was the hardest. The night before I'd gone to bed with my men and they'd hugged me all night long. I had been worried about having them both in my bedroom, especially with the children around, but Mum told me not to worry about it. They needed to see the love around the house. They needed to see the support we all gave each other, and she was right.

Dressed in a knee-length black dress, I walked from the bedroom to the kitchen where Talon, Blue, Clary, Mum, Zara and the kids were all dressed in their best clothes. Even Talon and Blue had on suits, something I thought I would never see, except for the day they got married. Which was coming up for Blue and Clary.

Blue and Clary hugged me tightly. Clary pulled back and gave me a sad smile as the front door opened and in walked my men.

Goodness. My hand went to my chest. They had always looked amazing, no matter what they wore, but that day they were also in suits and they looked incredible.

"Everything organised at the compound?" Mum asked. We had decided to have Dad's wake at the compound. It was the biggest and best place for it. Dad did love going there.

"Yeah, Nance. Simone's there with some brothers organisin' the whole thing."

Simone. She'd been wonderful. When my men weren't with me, she was.

"Good." Mum smiled. As she walked past me to the front door, she stopped, took my hand and gave it a squeeze. "You have the perfect people surrounding you, Josie. I'm so glad."

"I am too." I nodded, kissed her cheek and followed her out the front door to the car.

When we pulled up to the funeral home, I wasn't sure we would find a park, the area was surrounded with Harleys and other vehicles. We drove past many familiar faces, Vi, Travis, Warden, Griz and Deanna with their baby boy, Nickolas. Nary was there with Stoke, Malinda and Josh. Also Mrs Cliff showed, alongside her was Dallas, Dive, Killer, Ivy, Dodge and many more biker brothers.

Talon parked his car first in the three reserved spots left. He had Zara and the children in it. Next was Blue's, in it with him was Clary, Mattie and Julian. Our car was last to park, Caden had been driving with Eli in the front next to him and I was in the back, holding Mum's hand.

We got out of the car. Maya came over and took Mum's other hand. Mum smiled down at her grandchild, lifting their joined hands and kissing it.

Making our way in, we received a lot of sorrow-filled messages as we passed by many people. Mum sat up in the front on the end. I sat behind her in the middle of my men, while the rest of our family surrounded Mum. Where everyone else sat I didn't take notice because Talon suddenly appeared on the podium standing at the mic and next to Dad's coffin. The lid was closed, which I was grateful for.

The day before, it had been our own family viewing. I hated it was called that. We went to the funeral home to see Dad laying to rest in his coffin, to say our final goodbye. If

Caden and Eli hadn't been with me when it was my turn in the room with him, I would have lost it.

It hadn't been my dad in that coffin.

There was nothing left of *him* inside his body and feeling that, feeling the loss all over again, was like a hand sunk into my chest and squeezed my heart, shredding it into tiny pieces.

Eli carried me out of the room. My men then took me straight home where I curled into a ball and cried myself to sleep.

Talon cleared his throat in the mic and the room quieted.

"The usual ritual would be to have the reverend up here talkin' about Richard. Only Rich didn't want some stranger up here ramblin' on about some shit, about him and his life." Talon turned his head to the reverend. "Sorry," he muttered, bowing his head. The reverend smiled and nodded. "Richard had come to me a long time ago and said if anythin' happened to him, he wanted me up here talkin' about him." Talon smiled. "He also knew Nancy would hate it 'cause of my slang. He wanted one last word in." Mum snorted and shook her head as Talon smiled down at her.

"Richard Alexander was a good man. He was the best of the best and an honorary brother to the Hawks club." Talon waited while the shouts, cheers and clapping from his biker brothers stopped. "He took care of his own with everythin' he had. He loved his children with his whole heart. He'd be sad that he's gone and won't get to meet the rest of his grandkids, because his grandkids meant the world to him, like his own kids did. Richard will be missed by many people, but more by his family. The world won't be the same without him." He cleared his throat. "While we take a look at his past, let's listen to one song that Rich enjoyed." He nodded to someone, and the screen to the left of Talon started showing pictures of Dad. The speakers played "Bad to the Bone" by George Thorogood. People smiled, some laughed, but most cried.

Once the song ended, Mum kissed Maya on her head and stood, making her way up next to Talon. My eyes stayed on Maya, who also stood and moved in between Julian and Mattie. There she cuddled in. Zara smiled sadly at her and nodded, then placed her arm around Cody, whose whole body was shaking. Surprisingly, the twins were being good. Though, I guessed, in their own way, they knew the day wasn't a good one.

Mum stood on the podium, wiped her tears and stepped up to the mic. "My husband, my pain in the backside, my… as Richard would have said, my better half has left this world. He's left many wonderful memories." She paused as her bottom lip wobbled and fresh tears showed in her eyes. I squeezed tightly on to my men's hands. "Richard would want his children and our grandbabies to know… he would want you all to know that he's not far from you. Even now I'm sure he's looking down and telling me to stop my blubbering." She smiled fondly. "However, he knew I was never capable of it. He didn't care that I blubbered on about things. He just liked to tease, but all the teasing was out of love." She took a deep breath and looked to the roof.

"Richard Alexander, you wait for me. I will always love you. No man could compare to you. Ever." After a shuddering breath, she finished with, "I love you, my one true love."

I watched as Talon nodded to someone again and the speakers filled with Pink's "True Love". A giggle left my mouth and then it turned into a sob. I reached my hand out to my sister's shoulder. Her hand came up to touch mine briefly as I watched her own shoulders shake with grief.

Over the screen, more pictures showed of Dad, only that time they were of him with his family, with his grandkids and children. Each one was like a knife to the heart because they showed how much of a great man he was and how much he would be missed.

How much it hurt that he was gone.

My knees came up to the seat and I curled my body into them. My chin resting on my knees as I cried and watched the pictures flashing across the screen. Coldness was overtaking my body. I couldn't stop shaking. My men, my sweet men, knew what I was feeling and tried, with their arms at my back, rubbing some warmth into me. Only I knew it wouldn't work.

Nothing would work.

My body was feeling the loss of my dad.

My brain was screaming at how unfair it all was.

And my heart ached like a piece of it had been torn away.

When Mum sat back down, I slowly reached out to her as she brought Cody into her side while he cried. Running a hand over her back, she looked to me and smiled sadly. I had to remember I wasn't the only one feeling the way I was. I wasn't the only one feeling his loss.

Caden and Eli moved. They stood. Eli was already in the aisle and Caden was stepping around me before I started to panic. No, I needed my men.

Caden leaned in, took my hand and whispered, "We'll be with you soon." He gestured with his head to Dad's coffin where Talon, Blue, Griz, Killer and Stoke were already standing.

It was time for Dad to go.

He wished to be cremated.

Looking up to Caden, I nodded. He kissed my cheek and turned. As soon as he stepped out of the way, I felt someone take my hand, Mattie, and then someone was at my side. Nary. Before I left Ballarat, Nary and I had become fast friends. Having her beside me helped, but nothing could have prepared me for the next song or watching the men carry our dad out of the funeral home.

The speakers filled with Mariah Carey and Boyz II Men singing "One Sweet Day".

I crumbled into my friend's arms while holding my brother's hand as we followed Dad's casket out to the waiting car.

CHAPTER TWENTY-ONE

JOSIE

*T*oo soon we were at the compound. After walking out of the funeral home, and after the car had driven away to the crematorium, I was soon whisked away from Nary, into my men's arms. Mum decided to drive with Maya and Cody, while the twins went with Blue and Clary. When we arrived, the atmosphere was sad even though the sun shone. The compound, a usually busy, laughing, happy place, was now one where people walked around talking quietly with sober expressions. We mourned Dad, but the day shined over such a wonderful man.

My tears had dried up and I was making my way around the side of the compound when Nary called out.

Turning, I smiled as she walked quickly our way. I

looked back to my men and said, "Why don't you both go through. I'll be in there soon."

"Is that code for you wanting to talk to Nary about us?" Eli teased.

"Yes." Nary smiled as she stopped beside me.

Eli chuckled while Caden smirked. He quickly kissed me and started for the tall side gate. Eli slid his hand to my waist, winked and said, "Make sure you talk us up real good, babe." Then he kissed me and followed Caden.

Nary, taking my hand in hers, brought my attention away from my men and back to her smiling face. She waited until a few stragglers walked out the back of the compound before saying, "I'm so happy to see you're cared for by not only one but two men." Then her smile slipped. "It's sad Richard won't get to see more of it."

Licking my dry lips, I nodded. "It is."

"Still, he knew, and from what Stoke told Mum, he was very happy about it. He said he knew you were meant to be loved and fiercely so. He was happy that he got to know you'd be taken care of."

Hugging her, I said, "Thank you." Pulling back, I asked, "What's been happening with you? It's been too long since we've emailed last."

She shrugged. "Just the same really."

"How were the exams?" Nary was in her final year at high school. She was still contemplating on where to attend uni the following year.

"Good, I think at least."

"Have you picked a university?"

She laughed. "No, but I'm close."

I hesitated before asking, "How are things with Saxon?"

She groaned. "The same. He doesn't want anything to do with me. Besides, he's moving soon."

"I heard. So… there is always a chance you could attend my uni?" I smiled.

She grinned, shrugged and looked to the ground. "I'm not sure. It's hard to like someone who wants nothing to do with you… who sleeps with everything he can get his hands on and ignores the only one who would care for him."

Sighing, I touched her shoulder. "One day he'll come around."

Shaking her head, she said, "I doubt it and you never know, by the time that happens, I could have moved on." She laughed then. "At least then Stoke would be happy. I've lost count of the times he's told me to get over the undeserving little shit."

I threw my head back and laughed. Stoke would say that. He was very protective of Nary and Josh. I brought Nary in for another hug. "Thank you, you always did know what to say to make me smile."

"Same with you," she whispered and pulled back. "At least I know all I have to do is talk about my sucky love life."

"I'm sure it won't be sucky for much longer. Someone will see your worth and sweep you off your feet."

"Just like your guys have with you," she teased.

Laughing, I nodded. "Yes, just like my guys."

"Two men, Josie. Two!"

Biting my bottom lip, I blushed. "Every day I wake

thinking of how lucky I am. It helps that they get along so well. They've accepted that I couldn't choose between them."

"*So* lucky." She sighed giddily.

"I know."

"Not for long," a new voice snarled.

Nary and I jumped and turned to the entrance of the car park of the compound.

No.

Not today.

Not any day.

"You come with me now or I start shooting," Cameron ordered and raised his gun high, pointing it right at Nary.

"Don't," I pleaded and stepped in front of Nary. My heart pounded in my ears, my hands shook as I held them out in front of me.

"Then come with me." He held out his other hand toward me.

"Why? Why do this, Cameron? Do you know what today was for me? Do you even care?"

"No, I don't care that your dad died. Perfect opportunity for me. You're all I have ever wanted and I get what I want… one way or another." He sneered. "Now walk toward me and I won't have to hurt anyone."

"Why did you kill your dad and Caden's mum?"

Please, please someone walk back out the front. Please.

"We'll talk about that later," he snapped.

"No. I-I can't go with a person who's willing to kill people." I gulped and stepped back into Nary more.

"Don't you see? I had to do it. They were worthless, disgusting people. Now come." He shook his hand in front of him.

"Can I, please, can I just say goodbye to people?"

"No!" he snarled and then caught himself. "You will not go to those men again. They're nothing, Jo-Jo. I'm more than them. I can provide for you. You'll be happy with me."

"But—"

"Josie," he growled. "Come now or your friend won't be the only one I shoot today. I'll walk out the back and open fire on everyone, even if I get shot in the process."

No, God, no, the kids. Mum, my family. My men.

"Don't, Josie," Nary pleaded and grabbed my arm. She knew I wouldn't risk anyone else.

Turning to her with tears in my eyes, I smiled sadly and said, "I have to."

"No, no, you don't. Please, don't do this." She leaned in and whispered, "I'll scream. The men will come, they will."

I cupped her cheek and wiped her tears with my thumb. "But not before you get hurt. I can't let that happen. Not when I can stop it. Seek help after I'm gone—"

"Josie, now," Cameron barked behind me.

"My men will hunt him down. They *will* find me," I whispered to Nary. Turning, I stepped up to Cameron. He took my hand and started for the entrance.

"No," I heard Nary whisper behind me. "No!" she screamed.

"Nary, don't," I yelled, but it was too late. She grabbed at Cameron and they struggled. I tried to get in and help her, but I was knocked backward, my bottom hitting the ground hard. "Nary," I screamed before the gun was fired.

With wide eyes, I watched as Nary fell to the ground.

Blood.

Everywhere.

So much.

Blood covering Nary's face dripped onto the gravel ground.

I was hurled up and over a shoulder, jolted with every running step Cameron took.

PICK

Standing out the back of the compound with Eli, Saxon and Stoke just talking about random shit. But my eyes were glued to the side gate waiting for our woman to walk through with Nary by her side.

"You ready to make the move, brother?" Eli asked Saxon.

"Yeah, more than ready." Saxon nodded. He probably needed the break from Ballarat. Too many bad memories were here for him from having a fucked-up father like his.

Bloody lucky Stoke took him under his wing and got him out.

Saxon was a good brother, a mean motherfucker who didn't take shit any longer. He had the body to back it all up as well. Since joining the Hawks, he'd trained hard at the gym to gain the muscle. He was a big fucker now and everyone outside Hawks knew not to screw with him.

Still, we gave him shit all the time, but he knew we were just playing with him. That was what brothers were for. He soon learned and gave just as much shit back.

What was on the tip of my tongue was to ask him about his situation with Nary. Everyone knew she had the hots for him, but for some reason, he was standoffish with her. I had only one thought why and that thought was standing next to him. Stoke would skin him alive if Saxon fucked with his daughter, and Saxon knew it. He respected Stoke, looked up to him, which was probably why he steered clear of Nary.

It was too bad. Our woman was sure Nary and Saxon would be great together. I didn't really give a fuck, but I wanted my woman happy in every way and I hated it when she talked about Nary and Saxon and got a frown on her face because Saxon was being a dick.

"How're things in Melbourne?" Stoke asked after he took a pull from his beer.

"Last I spoke with Memphis, not good. The Venom club are being cunts tryin' to take business away from ours, opening a club just down the road from one of Talon's clubs," I said with a glare.

"Talk on the street is they're also dealin' in sellin' women," Stoke said.

"Fuck," Eli growled.

"Damn straight. That's why Talon not only has you two stayin' there, but why Saxon, Dallas, Dive and Dodge are there," Stoke informed us.

"Understandable," I said with a nod.

"Fuckin' lucky we got Lan as well," Eli added.

"Yeah, and apparently, Talon's asked Warden to get to Melbourne. Wants state-of-the-art cameras at all businesses. Doesn't trust anyone but Warden to do it."

"That fucker can fix up anythin'," Saxon said.

"Hey, guys," Malinda said as she walked up and claimed her man with an arm around his waist. Stoke looked down at his woman and touched his lips to hers. She smiled up at him. "Have any of you seen Nary?" she asked.

"Yeah, she's out the front with Josie, I—"

Everything stopped.

Everyone stood still.

"Nary," we heard screamed and then... fuck, then a gunshot sounded in the calm air.

Everything sprang back into action. Men hustled women and children inside.

"No," Malinda whispered. She started for the side gate. Stoke grabbed her and ordered her to the kids. I was already moving, rounding the corner. I ran through the gate and what I saw turned my blood cold.

Nary was on the ground, fucking blood everywhere on her and Josie was over Cameron's shoulder. He was making a run for it. "Stop," I yelled and started sprinting toward them.

All I saw was fury and a need.

A need to save our woman.

"Fuck!" Saxon bellowed behind me. "Fuck."

Cameron turned and fired.

A pain stabbed me in the neck. I stopped.

How could I stop?

I had to get to Josie.

Still, my feet were firmly set on the ground. My hand went to my neck and when I pulled it back there was blood on it.

Shit.

Looking up, I saw Cameron deposit Josie on her feet beside him. She took one look at me and screamed with anguish.

My mouth moved, but nothing came out. *Precious* was on my lips before I took my last breath and fell to the ground.

ELI

I was just behind Saxon when we got around the side, and a part of me turned to stone when my eyes landed on Nary on the ground, her blood being soaked up by the gravel. And then as Saxon roared, "Fuck!" my eyes found Josie over Cameron's shoulder.

Motherfucker.

The sound of a gun being fired hit my ears. I froze, but then my body jump-started and my eyes raked over Josie to see if she was hit. She hadn't. Cameron was standing her on her feet. They went to Saxon now on the ground beside Stoke and Nary, cursing, whispering and praying.

And then… fuck me. Fucking hell. My eyes landed on Caden as his body hit the ground.

Cameron took a screaming Josie into his arms and ran again.

"What the fuck?" Talon snarled from somewhere.

My feet took me to Caden, I knelt beside him.

"Fuck, fuck, fuck." Blood dripped out of his neck.

"Brother?" Blue said before touching Caden's neck. "No pulse."

No. Christ. No, no.

"Fix him," I growled low. "Fix him now. I'm gonna go get our woman back."

"Billy," Blue uttered. "It's too late."

"No!" I roared. "Fix him, brother, fuckin' fix him."

He read something from me and he nodded. "Go get your woman," he said.

With a nod, I ran faster than I had ever ran before. Footsteps behind me thumped on the concrete, echoing with my own. I knew it was Saxon and probably Talon. Both of them would want payback.

Not as much as I did.

"There, go light, go in and get the fucker," Talon ordered, pointing out Cameron as he rounded a corner down the street.

I took off into a neighbouring backyard. With a leap, I was over their fence and coming up the side of the house Cameron was on. My gun in my hand, I snuck low. No sound other than Josie's crying and Cameron cursing.

I had to get her back.

We needed our light.

Caden... holy Christ, my chest hurt. He had better be breathing when we get back.

Talon and Saxon had obviously turned to smoke and was coming in from their own way. I peeked around the house and saw Cameron, with shaking hands, trying to unlock a car. Josie crumbled to the ground sobbing.

But then.

Jesus. It was as if something had snapped inside her.

Josie turned her face from the ground up and glared at Cameron's back.

She bounded up. Her fists flew into his back. He fell into the car and she pounded into him yelling over and over, "You bastard, you killed him, you killed Nary. You bastard. You bastard. No more. No more."

Cameron turned to hit her. I dove behind the fence. I didn't want him to see me yet. Josie blocked the slap to her face and shoved with all her strength into his chest. He stumbled back, his hands out to steady himself. His gun dropped to the ground.

They both eyed it but Josie got to it first.

She took a step back and raised the gun.

"You deserve to die. I just lost my dad. I just saw you shoot two people I love. You deserve to die."

"Jo-Jo—"

"No," she screamed. Her hands shook as she held the gun.

"Sweetheart," I said quietly, standing. I jumped the fence

and was at her side in seconds. I knew her stance. I knew her thoughts. She was ready to take his life.

One hand to her shoulder, my other hand trailed slowly down her arm to her hands, and I wrapped my hand around hers on the gun.

"Babe," I uttered.

"Eli," she sobbed. "Caden?"

Jesus.

"I don't know."

"Eli," she uttered. "C-Caden?"

"He didn't have a pulse when I left."

She shook her head. "No," she cried. "No. No one will take from us again. No more," she declared before she fired the gun, hitting Cameron square in the chest. Shock marred his face as he stared down at his chest.

Saxon showed, took Cameron to the ground and hit him over and over. If the gunshot wound didn't kill him soon, Saxon would.

Talon, Griz and Killer appeared. They would handle things. They would clean everything up.

I had to take care of our woman.

My life.

My light.

And then… then we would get back to our other light. Caden.

Hopefully.

Fuck.

EPILOGUE

ONE MONTH LATER

I stood at the grave and I couldn't stop the tears flowing from my eyes. My heart ached. It wasn't fair. None of it was fair. If I'd known he was going to die, I would have... what? Spent more time with him, loved him stronger, and shown him what he meant to me more.

"He knew you loved him," Eli said, coming to stand beside me and taking my hand. All I could do was nod. It still felt all too fresh. I wanted to be happy with Eli by my side, but I couldn't. At that time, sadness had dragged me down deep into her hell pit to play with me.

Pain because he no longer was on the earth, surfaced once again.

Feeling the pain for the last month was nothing new.

However, standing there before his grave brought every-thing back.

"Sweetheart, it will get easier."

Would it?

I wasn't sure, but I had to believe it for our future.

Mum was finally able to go a day without crying. Nary was recovering after her first plastic surgery attempt. Still, she would always have a scar from the side of her lip up to her cheek bone. She didn't blame me for it, even though I blamed myself. Her life would be different from now on and I found it hard knowing that I was the cause. I would do anything for my friend. I hoped she knew it. I'd told her if she ever needed anything from me, I was there for her. I think the one thing that upset her deeply was that Saxon had left to join the Caroline Springs charter. She had been in love with him since she was sixteen. I truly hoped he would see the error of his ways and find his way back to her... or, I could even bring her to Melbourne with us one day. That was something to think about.

We were heading back to Melbourne, to our new home. I had many things to look forward to. Knowing my family would visit helped, and knowing I would make it back to Ballarat all the time helped. I had a plan at least and maybe that plan would help dull the pain.

Again, I could only hope.

Once we were settled into our house, I would head back to uni to finish my degree and then I would find a job and be able to do what I'd always wanted to do.

Time to move on... it didn't matter that the sorrow would follow. I welcomed it. It meant I wouldn't forget.

"You know I'll always be here for you," Eli said. I wrapped my arms around his neck and nodded. He would. He was wonderful like that and he loved me like I loved him. Never would I feel alone, never would I feel threatened.

Not when I had him.

"We'll always be here for you." And Caden. I had my men and we'd been through our own hell, but we survived. It was time to show Dad I could continue with life.

Shifting, I took Caden into my arms, but not before I eyed his scarred neck.

I'd nearly lost him. That thought still scared me.

I looked over his shoulder to Dad's grave.

Dad

I love you. I'll miss you every day, but I want you to know I'm happy.

And it was because of you I could be happy.

Never had I felt so much love because of what you and Mum did.

Never could I have wished for such wonderful parents because I didn't believe they existed.

They did.

And you were it.

You were my friend, my adviser, my counsellor and my dad.

I'll miss you, Dad.

Forever.

"Let's head home, yeah?" Caden asked.

I looked from him to Eli and smiled. I took a hand of each man I loved and we walked toward our future together.

CHAPTER ONE

WILLOW

"Come on, Low, you need a night out. When was the last time you got laid?" my co-worker, from the small supermarket we worked at together, questioned as she stood at her empty register. Thank God I was also free of customers in the run-down, rarely busy supermarket because Lucia went on. "You need a good shag, woman. Everyone can see how tense your arse is."

I giggled and shook my head at her. "Babe, why're you so worried about my arse? *I'm* fine with not getting any, so *you* shouldn't worry about it, either." I sent her an eye roll before picking up a new magazine to read.

"You work too hard, always askin' for extra shifts. You have no fun, and a no-fun Willow is a dull bitch. I want, just one day, to come to work and you tell me about a good poundin' you got the night before."

"Pfft! Aren't your own adventures enough to keep you occupied?" I asked, thumbing through the 'Who's Wearing What' section.

"I don't have enough goin' on in my life since bein' with Alex. I need to live through you now, girl, unless I cheat on my man. You wouldn't want that, would you? It'd be your fault if I cheated."

Snorting, I said, "You're so full of it. As if you would cheat on Alex. He dotes on you like you're a queen. Why'd you want to ruin that? Plus, like you said, he's magical in bed. Now *that's* something I've never experienced." Sighing, I put the magazine back and grabbed another. My sex life was, and always had been, non-existent. I was a twenty-two-year-old, born-again virgin. 'Born again' because I'd only had one lover, which lasted long enough for him to take my V-card and leave, never to be seen again. Not that Lucia knew that. I shuddered at the thought if she found out my snatch hadn't any visitors for the last six years. She'd probably organise a 'losing your V-card second time around' party, lining up several men to knock out that pesky grown-over-again hymen.

I glanced up at her and then back down before continuing. "And you know why I have to work my arse off. I need out of my cousin's house. I need to make a life for myself."

Living with a cousin I hardly knew, despite being there for two years, was something I never thought I'd do. There were so many contributing factors to why I was still there.

Like two years ago, the first time I tried to leave my high-on-ice parents' house only to find I couldn't because they'd stolen from me. After saving my arse off, I'd decided it was NL day, as in New Life day. I went to the bank to collect the hard-earned money, only to discover my account was dry. My parents had stolen my money so they could get high and invest in their own little pharmacy. An ignorant error on my behalf, having them added to my account in case they needed extra money for food and such. I'd left school at the age of sixteen so I could work and get out of my parents' house. It took me until I was twenty to have enough cash to make the escape. I didn't hate them for it, though.

I couldn't. They were my parents.

I was annoyed. No, that wasn't right. I was pissed. I wanted to string them up by their toes on the clothesline and beat them senseless, but I didn't.

They were neglectful parents, but they weren't so bad. They didn't beat me. They weren't mean to me nor did they abuse me. They simply didn't care enough about their child.

Ever since my younger sister drowned when I was six, ice became more important than anything to my parents. I cooked, cleaned, and did my own homework without any help. I raised myself. So even though I didn't hate them, I'd felt nothing when they died two months after I'd turned twenty. Unsurprisingly, they'd OD'd from an experimental batch gone wrong. I'd lost both my parents in one night, yet I spilled no tears to grieve for them.

I felt nothing.

My apathy wasn't because they'd left me with nothing; I had no money and no place to stay, so I was evicted. I was sure my lack of concern was because they didn't care enough about their only living daughter which caused me, in turn, to not care about them.

I still wasn't sure if that made me a bad person. The only saving grace at the time was the fact that my cousin, Colton, had turned up the day after their deaths and offered me some help. Not having many friends I could rely on, or any other family, I had no choice but to take him up on his offer. I didn't want to live on the streets and fend for myself. So even though Colton was practically a stranger, I had limited options but to trust him.

At least it worked out. Colton kept to himself. We shared the house, but honestly, we hardly saw each other. I was always busy working and he was busy...doing whatever he did. I'd asked questions about him, but it seemed he wasn't willing to share too much. I prayed every night I hadn't moved in with a serial killer. He never gave off the vibe he'd like to hack me up into tiny pieces, thankfully. He *was* my cousin, after all, and he was kind enough to look out for me. Still, I bought a lock for my bedroom door. However, what helped was that over the two years, he was more like a weird reclusive housemate than a family member. He'd moved me into the house he inherited from his father. My uncle had been rich, *very* rich, and left everything to Colton. I never really knew my uncle. He disowned my family, his drugged-up brother. I couldn't blame him, really; I'd been ashamed, as well.

Despite a pretty peaceful two years, I was ready to move out and stand on my own two feet. Excitement thrummed through me every time I thought about having a place of my own, followed by a giddy feeling in my stomach. Even though Fate had thrown me a crappy deck by bringing me into a world where the people who *were* my family didn't care an ounce about me, I was proud of the person I'd become. I strived to be better each day, to be nothing like my parents, where through the struggles of life, I didn't turn to alcohol or drugs and things were looking up. Finally, I was escaping the deep doo-doo that'd been thrown my way.

It was a new beginning for me, and I couldn't wait.

Shrugging the thoughts away, I continued talking to Lucia and flipping through the pages. "You never know, when I'm finally on my own two feet and in my own place, maybe I could find my own Alex. Or even start to have some fun by getting down and dirty with some stranger who would cause my girly parts to sing a hymn…" I stopped because I got the eerie feeling Lucia and I weren't alone. I looked up from the magazine to find a fine specimen of man standing in the doorway of the supermarket. Gorgeous, blondish-brown messy hair, ocean-blue eyes, and a large frame, which I guessed was popping with toned muscles, he wore dark jeans that hugged his firm thighs. I found myself wishing he would turn around to give us a show of his butt while shaking it. Combining that with a tight black tee and leather jacket, I was losing grip on reality and wondered if I'd somehow knocked myself out.

Then it all came back to me, the last words said from my

mouth. I blushed and prayed that the sinful man hadn't heard. Yet his smirk and wink as he walked past told me he had. I wanted to curl into a ball under my counter and pretend I wasn't there.

"Willow," Lucia said.

"Yes?" I sighed.

"Can you get me a mop?"

Dragging my reluctant eyes away from a *sweet* tush, I looked to her to see she was still watching the walking sin. "Why?" I asked.

She grinned wickedly before saying, "Because I just creamed my panties and made a puddle on the floor while watchin' that damn fine man walk in here."

"Lucia." I gasped and quickly looked down the aisle where my fantasy man had walked. He was no longer in sight. "You can't say that stuff out loud."

"Oh, girl, I can and I will." Then she laughed. "At least it wasn't me who said I was gonna get down and dirty and have my girly parts sing as he walked in."

"Snap, he heard?"

"Sure did." She grinned.

Standing up straight, I looked to the clock. It was past seven at night which meant... "At least I don't have to embarrass myself more. It's time for me to go." I smiled, grabbed my bag from under the counter and walked over to Lucia for a quick hug goodbye.

"Sure you don't wanna stay? He may offer himself up for your dirty ride."

Snorting, I said, "No. I think I'll keep him in my fantasy drawer."

"Have smokin' dreams tonight, girl."

Waving over my shoulder, I said, "Oh, I will." I turned to wink, but didn't get there. Instead, I squeaked when I spotted Mr Sin himself standing at her counter. Lucia burst out laughing as I practically ran from the shop.

The bus ride home seemed to take longer than any other day. It didn't help that I was sweltering and the man next to me was enjoying being in my personal space, making me hot and uncomfortable. I contemplated if the air-conditioning on the bus was even working. I felt the beast of a man beside me look down at me once again. I didn't want to meet his gaze in case he wanted to start up a conversation.

Oh. Snap. He shifted and a whiff of BO caught my nose, nearly making me gag.

Gripping my bag closer to my chest, I closed my eyes and rested my head against the window. *Come on, stop, come on.* The whole ride threatened to put a dampener on my good mood. Yet, I still couldn't wait to get home and tell my cousin I was moving out. I'd even found a small apartment in the paper that morning. I rang the realtor on my break and I would head there the next day to take a look. Everything appeared promising, though. A couple of weeks and I'd be on my own.

A smile lit my face. Yes, even with the scent of BO in my nose, I could still smile. It was as though nothing could take away my happiness.

Finally, my stop came. I squeezed past Stinky and felt a pinch on my arse.

Turning quickly, I pointed in his pudgy face and snapped, "Would you like to have babies one day?"

His eyes widened, but he nodded.

"Then don't ever do that again to any female or one day, your balls will be sliced off by some pissed-off woman. You're just lucky I'm in a good mood or it would be me."

I made my way down the aisle and off the bus. Heck, the small breeze in the humid air was better than that rubbish bus trip.

Around the corner of the bus stop was Colton's house. Walking up the path, I reached the house and unlocked the door. Thick heat greeted me, letting me know my cousin wasn't home. Once I turned the air-conditioner on, I made my way down to my room and dropped my bag. After a quick shower in the bathroom at the end of the hall, I dressed in a sleeveless tee and denim shorts. Feeling more comfortable out of my work gear, I walked into Colton's study munching on an apple.

I needed access to his computer to transfer some money from my chequing account to my savings account.

His laptop was already open on his desk and with a quick wiggle of the mouse, it came to life. I logged in and smiled to myself. After today's wages, there would be exactly what I needed to make the move.

My apple slipped from my hand to the floor.

No.

Not again.

It was empty, except for fifty cents.

Where was my money?

My heart tightened in my chest. Tears formed in my eyes, but I wiped them away.

I searched through the transfer information and discovered Colton's name as recipient. There had to be an explanation. There had to be. He wouldn't do it to me, not after knowing what my parents did. He wouldn't. He couldn't be that heartless.

The one person I had left in my life I couldn't trust, either.

No. Hold out hope. Something could have happened. There had to be a good explanation on why my goddamn money was gone. There had to be.

He wouldn't need my measly savings. He had an inheritance worth hundreds of thousands.

I searched through the help information, trying to see if there was a way to stop the transfer. Confused by the small print swimming before my eyes, I took the time to frantically search through his document files. I lucked out when I found his own bank sign-in details in a Word document.

A moment later, I stared at the screen and his bank balance. His account sat at zero.

God. I really, *really* was stupid.

It was then I heard the front door open. I pushed the chair back and strode from the office, down the hall and into the living room where Colton was shouldering his bag off.

"Where is it?" I asked, ashamed my voice quivered.

"What?" he asked with a smile.

"My money. Your money."

His face darkened. "You been in my study, woman, my account? What the fuck you think you doing in there? In my fucking business?" He stalked towards me.

For a second, fear clawed its way through me. "Colton, my account is empty, transferred to you. Your account is fucking empty." I kept my voice strong. "My money, where has it gone?"

Abruptly, just before he got to me, he stopped and smiled. "Don't you worry about a thing now. I have it all figured out. Everything will be fine, cuz." The gleam in his eyes told me everything would not be fine.

"I-I need my money, Colton. I'm moving out." My hands restlessly played with the bottom of my shorts to keep from picking the bastard up and throwing him out the window.

He laughed, shaking his head like I had said the funniest thing. "Sorry, cuz."

That didn't sound good. "About what?"

His head cocked to the side and he smirked over at me. I watched as his hand went behind him and he pulled a gun free, pointing it at me.

"What? No!" I took a step back. My hands out and up in front of me, my heart beat erratically in my chest. I didn't even know he owned a gun, or if he was smart enough to use it. "Colton, what's this about?"

Even when my heart was going haywire with panic, I wanted to wrap my hands around his throat and squeeze the life out of him. Better yet, I wanted to take that gun from him and shoot him in the balls. However, I did nothing but freeze.

"You see, I lost a bit of money. I like to gamble, and I gambled with the wrong people. I had to do something to save myself."

My stomach dropped. "What?" I whispered.

"I gave them all the money we had."

My arms went around my stomach. I gripped my sides as the hurt and betrayal bombarded me.

The only family member left on Earth turned on me for his own benefit.

Like my parents had.

I'd trusted him when he said he would support me.

He'd lied.

Like all my family seemed to do.

My money was gone. Colton's money was gone, and his fear was what brought my own fear on. Even though he looked smug, I could see the terror in his wide, twitching eyes. The people he'd played with were bad people.

"S-so, I'll, um, I'll just work harder and get some money back in." Like hell I would. I was out of there as soon as I could.

He sighed and shook his head. "My money and yours wasn't enough. I had to give them something else."

God. I closed my eyes and my head dipped forward. I was too scared to ask.

It seemed I didn't need to though because Colton supplied it. "You."

I was going to be sick. I was going to throw up all over

the carpet. My body shook with shock. Had I heard him right?

Lifting my head, opening my eyes, I asked in a quiet voice, "Me?"

"Yeah, cuz. Found a good buyer through some mates. They deal in slavery themselves, but when I showed them a picture of you, the biker wanted you for himself. Said he needed a good black bitch in his house taking care of shit." The sick shine in Colton's eyes when he explained he'd sold me was enough to know my owner would bring new, darker times with him. "He'll be coming by in a couple of hours. You just have to be a good girl 'til then."

He gestured with the gun for me to walk down the hall. I started and he followed, still talking, "There ain't no use running and going to the cops. He's in with them. Pays them off. I didn't want to do it. I was happy to help you out after your 'rents died, but I have to look out for myself over anything. You just happened to be staying here when things went down for me."

He reached out, grabbed the back of my hair and yanked it. I screamed in surprise and stumbled back before he shoved me sideways into his bedroom. I gripped his wrist, digging my fingernails in as he kept pushing me forward with force. I then stumbled into his en suite. He slammed the door behind me. A lock was snapped into place before I heard Colton say through the door, "Don't worry, cuz, it'll all work out." He laughed. "Though, even if it don't, I'll be a happy rich guy once again. I'd do fucking anything to have money under my belt, always."

I banged and kicked the door, screaming, "Let me out, Colton!"

"Now, stay quiet and I'll keep you breathin' until he gets here. Oh, and in case you get a hair-brained idea, there's no escaping through that window. Your fat arse wouldn't fit." I listened as he walked off chuckling.

My life, my pitiful life, would no longer be my own.

I refused to let that happen. I just didn't know how to make it possible.

I wanted to live, to be free and be who I was inside and out. No one had the right to own me.

For a little while, I sat on the cold floor and cried. Never once had I cried when my parents passed or when my uncle died. Never until then. Sobs racked my body. They came hard and I shook from the force. My head thumped painfully at my temples.

My life seemed doomed and I let myself wallow in self-pity, let the turmoil in my stomach take over and fill me with dread. How could it happen? How could my cousin be involved with people who sold women? Had I been a trusting fool from the start? Regardless, I never saw the signs. How could I when we hardly kept each other's company.

I wasn't sure how long I sat on the cold floor, but it was long enough to shake my stupid self and do something about my life *once again*.

I had to take the control back.

I had to try something, anything.

Fighting for my life was worth it. I'd done it many times. It was time to do it again.

With renewed energy, I stood from the floor and looked around and through cabinets but found nothing; he'd cleared everything out except for towels. I wasn't strong enough to take my cousin down forcibly when he would come for me, and no doubt, my *owner* would be there to back him up.

Instead, I looked to the small window again, and decided I had to try it at least. Turning on the shower to cover some noise, I quickly picked up the bath towel, wrapped it around my fist and punched the window. At first, I thought Colton would rush back in once he'd heard the glass shatter. However, my cousin, being the stupid fool he was, was probably sitting in front of the TV, drinking a beer with the surround sound up loud.

Moving quickly, so I could get as far away as I could before he noticed, I first placed my arms through the small window and wiggled my body against each corner, grazing it against the sides and shards that remained. Still, I didn't care. I needed out.

Standing on the toilet, I forced my body forward until my top half was out. Panic seized me as my hips got stuck. I prayed Colton wasn't right, that my arse wasn't too big.

I couldn't give up, though.

Shifting around, slicing more grooves into my skin, I managed to wiggle free. My body sank quickly to the rocky garden below the window, and I bit my lip to stop myself from crying out.

I didn't have the time to take in the pain.
I sprung up with determination and ran.

Chapter Two

EIGHT HOURS LATER

DODGE

Three months I'd been at the Hawks' Caroline Springs charter and shit had hit the fan. Not only were the Venom MC fuckers causing hell, but we had our own problem within our own club. Nothing we could prove, but we had our suspicions of someone within the club working against us and helping out the Venom MC instead. If that was the case and we found the dickhead in our own goddamn club backstabbing us and telling the Venom our every move, then whoever it was had better disappear before Dallas or I found them.

We were sick of our boss's nightclubs being ransacked, and wished to fuck Warden had already installed the cameras in the compound and garage. Then we could catch the bastards. But he was stuck in Ballarat dealing with his own shit. The Venom knew when one of Talon's nightclubs was unprotected. Or they'd draw brothers out from one club to another with false shit like the women being threatened, hold-ups or bomb threats.

Plans had to change. Brothers from the mechanical business were being over-worked while working backup at night at the clubs around our territory.

Things were in chaos. It was time to change it and take the control back.

It had been early when I walked into the compound. The mechanical business on the side of the building wasn't even open yet, which was good. Tired of fucking waiting on Warden, I was doing my own little installing. We needed to catch the snitch before the Venom cunts ruined everything.

Memphis had given me the go-ahead and those we trusted—Dallas, Saxon, Pick, Billy and Dive—knew I was setting up cameras that morning in the compound and then the garage.

It sucked that it'd come to not trusting a brother of Hawks, but we needed to weasel out the prick running his mouth off to someone in the Venom club.

At least things had settled down for Pick and Billy. They'd been back in Melbourne for a month. They'd moved into their own place with Josie. She was back at uni and they were enjoying each other. Fucking strange to me, the three of them together, but each to their own. I guessed it was whatever floated their boat and, if the three of them together was it, then so be it.

How in the fuck did it work, though?

My imagination would provide me enough pictures to go

through if they only starred Josie. She was fucking hot. But shit, I'd shut my brain down if it tried to get me to picture shit with her *and* my brothers. That crap was just not happening.

Switching on the last camera in the compound, I jumped down from the chair and placed it back where it belonged. It'd been a fucked-up day when Richard passed. It hurt people deep, and still so many were grieving for him. What made it worse was Talon had enough crap on his plate with his family's sorrow, and now he had all the shit in Melbourne on top of it. Which was why I was taking some slack off him and Memphis.

Memphis was a great president for the charter. He was a mean motherfucker when he had to be.

But I was ruthless.

If I wanted something, I saw to it and, if anyone got in my way, they'd better look the fuck out.

First on my agenda was to find the dick who thought he was man enough to play with the big boys and stab his brotherhood in the back.

Then I'd be dealing with some members of Venom. They needed to get the message that Hawks weren't to be fucked with. I'd relay that message any way I could—fists, knives or guns, I wasn't picky.

Dallas was keen to have my back and I was glad to have him there. He was just as merciless as I was. Together, with the help of our brothers who moved from Ballarat to Melbourne, we'd have the shit sorted and things would finally fucking calm down.

At least, I goddamn hoped.

After looking up at the hidden camera, I moved into the business side. Unlocking the door from inside of the compound to the mechanical area, I swung it open wide. It hit the wall with a bang.

That was when I heard it.

A small whimper.

"Hello?" I barked gruffly. Nothing but silence greeted me back. Hell, had I heard it? Shrugging, I moved over to the long metal table and dropped my shit down. Opening the bag, I took out the camera and turned, only to kick over a fucking stool and have it crash to the ground.

Another whimper.

"All right, who's there?" I called and quickly turned back to the table to put the camera away in the bag. Then I scanned the area.

Nothing looked out of place. Had a cat or some damned animal got in somehow before a brother had locked up?

A scuffle came from the left, and my eyes landed on a dark bare foot being dragged backward. Someone was hiding in the fucking corner of the room. The spot was small. It was between two benches, so whoever was in there was small in frame. Couldn't be a large motherfucker about to get his arse handed to him.

Slowly, I started forward. "You better come the fuck out," I demanded before peering around the corner of the bench. My eyes widened and I took a step back when scared, mossy-coloured eyes blinked up at me through a thick veil of curly black, scruffy hair.

"What the fuck?" I whispered.

279

The small woman pedalled her feet back on the ground, her hands holding her frame up as she tried to push herself against the wall more.

If she didn't have the look of some dirty, homeless woman, she'd be a stunner. Her skin looked silky smooth. It was the colour of milk chocolate and caused my eyes to stay glued to her. My gaze flicked to her legs, her body and her face. Never had I had an urge for a taste of chocolate until that moment. Well, except for the woman at the store I'd seen the previous day. My eyes widened again. Holy mother fucking shit, it *was* her. The cowering woman on the floor was the same woman as the one at the bloody store. I'd had an urge to go up and talk to her in the shop, but she'd quickly disappeared, embarrassed from what I'd caught her saying. Even when her words, soulful eyes and body intrigued me to want to know her more.

Composing my shock, I stepped forward. She squealed and closed her eyes tightly.

"Hey, hey. I won't hurt you," I said calmly with my hands out in front of me. She stopped moving and glanced up at me quickly, only to avert her eyes back to the floor in the next second.

Christ, how was I supposed to deal with this? Why was she here?

"What're you doin' here?" I asked as my eyes raked over her body. That was when I saw the blood. Her arms and legs were scraped to shit. The material of her tee and jean shorts didn't cover much of her body. How in the fuck did she get scraped up like that?

She must have felt me shift as I reached for my phone in the back pocket of my jeans because she shifted around restlessly and panic flashed across her features.

"I'm just gettin' my phone," I said and waved it out in front of myself. "I'll call the cops and—"

"No!" she screamed. She tried to stand, but her bare feet wouldn't support her. She cried out in pain and fell to her arse.

"S'okay, it's all right. Calm, little bird."

Little bird?

Maybe because she reminded me of an injured bird, all flighty and scared.

"Look," I reassured and sat on the ground in front of her, placing my phone on the filthy, concrete ground. "I won't call the cops, okay." She eyed the phone then gave me a small nod, her body sagging in relief. Did she recognise me, as well? "Is there anyone I can call for you?" I asked.

She shook her head once.

"Little bird, you can't—"

The door to the garage burst open and laughter reached our ears. The woman squealed, her arms winding around her knees. She buried her head in her arms, muttering and whimpering to herself about something I couldn't catch.

Jumping up, I started for the door as Slit, Muff and Handle stepped through. They were brothers to the Caroline Springs charter, brothers I was just getting to know, so I wasn't sure if I could trust them.

"Get the fuck out," I growled. They paused and eyed me.

"We've got work to do, arsehole," Muff said with a glare.

"Yeah, just because you think your shit don't stink and the boss man has a hard-on for you, don't mean you can tell us what to do," Slit barked.

"Slit," Handle was kind enough to warn.

Too late, though.

I was up in his face, pushing the dick backward and out of the room before he registered to fight back. The other brothers followed. "I don't give a fuck what you think 'bout me, but I have enough say to order you fuckers around. You do as I fuckin' well say. If you don't, I'll come see you in your dreams, and it won't be pretty." Glaring at the wanker in front of me, I finished with, "The shop is closed until I say further."

"Fuck off," Slit spat and stupidly added, "I could have you knocked out in seconds."

"Slit," Muff snarled. "Watch who you say shit to. Your brain ain't registerin' who your mouth is runnin' off to, dickhead." He shook his head at his friend. "That's Dodge."

Still close, with our chests touching, Slit stiffened. Now he knew the deep shit he just dug for himself. I had the highest kill count in Hawks. All charters included.

No one fucked with me.

I protected all.

"You get me now, pencil dick?" I asked with a smirk.

He nodded. I stepped back and ordered, "Shop is closed. You need to tell Memphis? Do it. Have him ring me, or when he gets here, he can come see me. For now, you two,"—I pointed to Muff and Handle—"guard the doors, inside and out. No one comes in there except

282

brothers who came from Ballarat." I thumbed towards the garage and then turned to Slit. "And you, get the fuck outta my sight."

"What's goin' on in there?" Handle asked.

"Not your business until I know I can trust you," I stated, and then walked back into the garage, slamming the door behind me.

Thinking of the scared woman caused me to sigh, my head falling forward, and I shook it.

Fuck. I'd just gone against brothers for a woman.

What in the hell was I thinking?

Even though I hardly knew the guys, they were still brothers. Slit, I couldn't give a fuck about, but I'd just admitted I wasn't trusting anyone around there. Which meant no fucker would think to open up to me and share shit.

And all for a fucking woman.

I swore, after seeing the shit boss man and my brothers in Ballarat went through for their women, I wouldn't get pussy-whipped like them.

Fuck it. I won't let it happen.

No woman comes between me and my brothers.

Tilting my head to the side, I glared down at the little bird who cringed and shivered on the ground. No woman was worth any trouble.

But Christ.

Maybe I'd been around the Ballarat brothers and their misses too long and had gotten soft-hearted, because something deep inside me knew I couldn't leave the woman like her on the floor. I couldn't turn my back on her. She needed help, and I had to give it.

Didn't mean I had to give her anything else.

I was too hard for that shit.

I didn't feel.

All I liked was to fuck a tight, wet pussy and do it hard.

What I needed to do was get her the fuck out of there and let someone else deal with her before my heart got caught in the trap like all the other bastards.

I strode over towards her. She whimpered when I bent down for my phone. "I won't fuckin' hurt you," I barked. "I'm not callin' the pigs, okay. Just someone who can help you. Someone I trust." After pressing a couple of buttons, I held my phone to my ear.

"Brother?" Pick answered.

"Bring Josie to the garage. I'm gonna need some help with a little bird."

"What the fuck you talkin' about?" he growled.

"Just do it," I snapped and hung up.

ACKNOWLEDGEMENTS

Hot Tree Editing—Becky, and her super-duper team, thank you for always being there for me and being amazing and easy to work with. Without a great team, like you ladies, I wouldn't have gotten the Hawks team out there for everyone to read. I honestly can't thank you enough.

Justine Littleton, I'm sure everyone knows by now I effing love you! Thanks for... being you!

Jeneane Johnston, Keeana Porter, Debbie Poole, Donna Pemberton, Jill D, Rebecca Allman and Susan Griffiths, thank you all for your help. You ladies are amazing. xx

Rachel Morgan, you, my sister, are fantastic. Even when you get bossy, I know I can always count on you and if I tell you to shut it, you do. Your help with the signings in Australia is always appreciated.

Thank you to my tool man and the kids. Taking on the change in our lives has been hard. I'm not always there now, but you have all been amazing and supported me along the way, even shoved me out the door for my US signings. I love you all.

Bloggers, you know who you are... the hard-working supporters of indie authors like myself. Thank you for always having our backs!

ALSO BY LILA ROSE

Hawks MC: Ballarat Charter

Holding Out (FREE) Zara and Talon

Climbing Out: Griz and Deanna

Finding Out (novella) Killer and Ivy

Black Out: Blue and Clarinda

No Way Out: Stoke and Malinda

Coming Out (novella) Mattie and Julia

Hawks MC: Caroline Springs Charter

The Secret's Out: Pick, Billy and Josie

Hiding Out: Dodge and Willow

Down and Out: Dive and Mena

Living Without: Vicious and Nary

Walkout (novella) Dallas and Melissa

Hear Me Out: Beast and Knife

Breakout (novella) Handle and Della

Fallout: Fang and Poppy

Standalones related to the Hawks MC

Out of the Blue (Lan, Easton, and Parker's story)

Out Gamed (novella) (Nancy and Gamer's story)

Outplayed (novella) (Violet and Travis's story)

Romantic comedies

Making Changes

Making Sense

Fumbled Love

Trinity Love Series

Left to Chance

Love of Liberty (novella)

Paranormal

Death (with Justine Littleton)

In The Dark

CONNECT WITH LILA ROSE

Webpage: www.lilarosebooks.com

Facebook: http://bit.ly/2du0taO

Instagram: www.instagram.com/lilarose78/

Goodreads:
www.goodreads.com/author/show/7236200.Lila_Rose

CPSIA information can be obtained
at www.ICGtesting.com
Printed in the USA
BVHW041855140521
607379BV00022B/315